THE FATES

THOMAS TESSIER

Dedicated to my parents
Armand "Pete" and Helen Tessier

PART ONE
THE PRESENCE

"… and the earth shall rise up against him."
– Job, XX, 27

CHAPTER ONE

"Improbable."

Dave Lutz, teacher of sophomore English at Millville High School, wrote the word on the blackboard. "Improbable. A nice easy one to start off with, okay?" Several hands shot into the air. "Miss Fratesi."

"Improbable means like impossible… right?"

"You're on the right track, but you haven't arrived at the station yet, I'm afraid." Lutz sat on the corner of his desk.

"Really impossible?" Janet Fratesi added quickly, her eyebrows arched hopefully.

"No, not quite. Someone else? Is your hand up, Mr. Nardello?"

"No, sir."

"I didn't think so, but it's nice to know you're still awake." Lutz pointed back to the written word. "Improbable. Improbable. Miss Evans."

"Improbable means something that is possible but highly unlikely."

"Thank you very much. Improbable is an adjective that means unlikely. We could have snow today, but since it's the eighth of June and it's very hot, we can say that a snowstorm is an improbable event. Unlikely. Got it?" Lutz stepped behind his desk and erased the word from the blackboard. "Let's try something a little harder this time. Aloof." Again he spelled the word out on the blackboard. Harder, he thought grimly. These kids are sixteen years old, and half of them don't even know what improbable means. Still, if they graduate from high school illiterate it won't be because I didn't try. "Aloof. Come on, don't any of you ever do the crossword-puzzle in the newspaper?"

"Mr. Lutz?"

"Yes, McNamara?"

"Is that related to a goof?" Ronnie McNamara grinned broadly at the chorus of chuckles he had earned.

"No, it isn't related to you at all." The chuckles turned to laughter. "All right now, does anyone have any idea what aloof means?" Jackie Evans raised her hand again and Lutz nodded to her.

"Does it mean far away, distant, or something like that?"

"It does mean something like that, Jackie. You must be the only person in this class who knows how to read. Aloof means distant or reserved as with someone who can't be bothered to associate with other people; someone who keeps to himself, you would call that person aloof."

"Hey, Mr. Lutz?"

"Hey what, McNamara?"

"Where does that word come from?" The youth settled back into his seat with a smart smile on his face.

"It comes from the dictionary, McNamara. Look it up. You do know what a dictionary is, don't you?"

"Oh yeah, sure."

"Good. Try opening it sometime."

"I just thought you might know."

"I hope you're writing all these words down, McNamara, because I may quiz you on them soon."

"I can see them on the blackboard. I got a photographic memory."

"Well, you didn't get the picture on the last exam. I hope you do between now and finals."

Lutz wiped the blackboard clean again. Sixteen years old and scarcely literate. What had he been like at that age? It was only a few years ago, nine to be exact, but it seemed far away. Probably just as silly and uncertain, overall, but he at least had known what improbable and aloof meant. Are kids getting by on less and less words? Is the every-day vocabulary people use shrinking? Maybe a subject for a nice smart little essay. Dazzle them in the teachers' lounge. But he knew he'd never write it.

"Let's try another word." He began writing again. Chalk: there would be a lot of that in his future. Chalk and vodka tonics.

"Tantamount. Anybody? Tantamount. Someone, try. Miss Marsh, what do you think it means?"

Leslie Marsh frowned with annoyance. She hadn't raised her hand, so why should Mr. Lutz pick her out of the thirty students in the room? It was unfair. "I don't know. Is it a special kind of horse?"

"No, it isn't," Lutz replied curtly. *Two hundred plus students in sophomore English, and I get the dogs.*

"Well I said I didn't know," Leslie Marsh muttered with an edge of defiance.

"Tantamount. Brooks, are you looking for something on the ceiling?"

"No, sir."

Well then, kindly join the rest of us down here. The word is tantamount and it refers to something that is essentially the same as some other thing. It implies an equality of value or effect. An example: it can be said of some of you people that to fail your final exams is tantamount to failing the whole year, because that is what would happen. Okay? Tantamount. Learn it."

A few students dutifully wrote down every word Dave Lutz spoke, but most made only a few brief notes and stared back at him. *Proceed. It's hard-going, but proceed. Only two more weeks and then summer break.* This time he didn't bother to erase the last word.

"Intrepid. Miss Diorio."

"Brave."

"That's right. Brave, fearless." He drew a line through tantamount and then another through intrepid. *It was something new to do.,*

"Raze. R-A-Z-E. Raze. Yes, Perkins?"

"Does it have something to do with demolition?"

"Yes, it can. You're close."

"Does it mean demolition?"

"First of all, Mr. Perkins, raze is a verb. Demolition is a noun. What does that tell you?"

"Oh, uh raze means to demolish something?"

"Good enough. Raze means to tear down something, like an old building, to demolish, to destroy, to level something to the ground. Raze, a nice short word. Watch the spelling." Lutz drew a line through the word and then glanced at the clock on the wall. Fifteen minutes to a cigarette.

"Hey, Mr. Lutz?"

"Yes, Nardello?" Lutz wasn't quite able to disguise the sound of surprise in his voice. Bernie Nardello hardly ever had anything to say.

"If the Leaning Tower of Pisa," Nardello pronounced it *pizza*, "fell over, would you say it was razed?"

"I wouldn't, no." Lutz paused for several seconds. "To raze is actively to tear down something not just something falling over by itself."

"Oh. I got ya now."

"Good for you. Now." Lutz turned to the blackboard. On second thought, it was time to erase the words again. With long sweeping strokes. Then he wrote. "Perspective." Lutz thought of his favorite passage from James Joyce's *Portrait of the Artist as a Young Man*, when Stephen Dedalus, with a few notes inscribed in his schoolbook, expanded his perspective from the classroom to the universe. "Perspective. Mr. Farley?"

"That's like a view, isn't it?"

"All right. What kind of view?"

"From far away?"

"Can anybody be more precise?"

"Mr. Lutz?"

"Deborah?"

"Is it when you're looking at paintings, like in a museum?"

"That's not what I'm looking for. Anyone else?" No more hands were raised. Still, the response was better than he had expected. "Perspective. A kind of view. It's when you look at one thing in relation to its surroundings, and not just in terms of that one thing. Listen. We're in a classroom at the moment and while we're here we tend to think in terms of this room, where we are and what we are doing here — those of us who aren't daydreaming. But let's put ourselves in perspective. Here is the classroom." Lutz drew a small square on the blackboard. "The classroom is in the school building." He drew a slightly larger square around the first one. "The school is in the town of Millville." Another, larger square. "Millville is in Connecticut." And another square. "…the United States… the planet Earth… the Solar System… the galaxy… it all depends on what your perspective is, or what kind of perspective you want to put on things… the relation of one object to another or several others… That is—"

Various school papers and drawings pinned to the bulletin board mounted on the wall near the classroom door suddenly began to flap, as if in a steady wind. But there was no wind, nor even a breeze. The weather was hot, muggy and still. Yet the papers were definitely flapping loudly now, and some of the sheets tore loose from the cork and were blown to the floor. Everyone in the room stared with wonder, including Dave Lutz. He put down the piece of chalk and walked across the room to the bulletin board. The papers stopped moving as he reached the spot.

Lutz noticed that the air seemed very cool.

Everything was in place.

Jim Donner took pride in his own sense of order. He was the neatest person he knew. At the Millville Post Office where he had worked for the past seventeen years, his section of the sorting room was easily the best organized. And it was always immaculate when he left at the end of the day. He loathed sloppiness; it was an abomination, an attack on the natural order of things. Through the years, he had suffered a good deal of ribbing and practical joking from his fellow workers, but it never really bothered him. Work was, after all, only work, and these things were to be expected. Jim Donner wasn't foolish enough to think he could change other people's ways. Although the idea had a certain abstract appeal (a perfectly neat world: think of it!) reform didn't interest him.

Chess did. He had played the game since he was fourteen, with, like so many addicts, considerably more passion than ability. Chess was the ultimate game, the only game. With its deep, hidden beauties, and its remorseless logic, it was the closest thing to absolute purity that Donner knew, and he loved it He played at the local club two nights a week, participated in six or eight large tournaments in the New England-New York area every year, and at home he studied chess, playing over the games of masters and grandmasters, for at least three hours each night. His chess library contained nearly 500 volumes, plus stacks of international magazines, journals, and bulletins all carefully catalogued according to his own special system.

The living room of Donner's small apartment had, many years ago, become his chess room. He had no family or relatives, and the few friends he occasionally had in were invariably fellow chess buffs. A table with a chess board and pieces stood in the center of the room with two chairs. A synthetic leather couch against one wall was the only other seating provided. There were three unmatched bookcases, a cheap tape recorder and a small pile of tapes. The carpet was grey and worn, without an underpad.

This evening Donner was home early. He had been in a club tourney and had lost his game in only seventeen moves. To a schoolboy—that made it worse. Snotty bastard. No manners. Why did kids think they had to be rude, nose-picking little monsters to be like Bobby Fischer? Donner threw his crumpled score-sheet on the table and went into the kitchen to pour a glass of iced tea. Calm down, play the game over, find the mistakes. He knew he had made several. Of course, he had started off at a slight disadvantage. The kid played a King's Gambit against him, an opening Donner was not overly familiar with. The Closed Ruy Lopez or the Nimzovich—now, these openings he knew twenty-odd moves deep, and was comfortable with them. But the brat's wide-open attacking play in a line Donner knew only superficially had completely unnerved him. It was an outdated gambit too, not worthy of a serious player, but obviously Donner would have to brush up on it. Didn't Fischer write a refutation of the King's Gambit years ago? He would have to dig it up.

Donner put on a ninety-minute reel of Vivaldi; baroque music seemed to go well with chess and it had a soothing effect on him. The first time, he went through the game quickly, noting only that he was in trouble by the sixth move and was in a virtually lost position by the tenth. Should have castled, he thought, as he reset the pieces and started play again. My king is caught in the open, subject to constant attack. He stopped at move seven and stared at the position for a long time. I'm pushing too many pawns trying to prove his opening unsound. The right idea but the wrong method. Then suddenly it seems all his pieces are in play and I'm tied up. What does *MCO* say? Probably to resign. He went to the bookcase, and took down a hefty volume entitled *Modem Chess Openings*. He went back to the board and began flipping through the book for the relevant section. Donner looked at the board and then back to the page again. Christ, I was out of the book on the third move. Bad, bad.

While he was studying the long grey column of figures in the book, the white king, on the far side of the board, fell over. Without thinking about it Donner picked up the piece and set it back on its proper square. Then he looked at it again. Odd. He was about to move ahead in the game a few moments later when the white king again fell over, this time rolling right off the table. Donner set the book down on the table, got up and retrieved the king from the floor. The pages of his *MCO* were flipping as if in a breeze and two other pieces fell over on the board and rolled back and forth on the squares. Donner put the white king back on the board and it fell over immediately.

"What the—"

Donner hadn't felt any wind. He turned to the two windows which looked out on Hoadley Street. They were half open, but his linen curtains hung slackly. Donner went and shut both windows. He turned at the clattering sound. The pages were still flipping. His score-sheet had blown onto the floor. Chessmen were scattered all over the table. For a brief second Donner thought they all looked blue. One piece flew through the air and bounced off his chest.

Police Chief Alvin Sturdevent leaned back and swiveled slowly in his desk chair, idly poking the yellow blotter in front of him with his letter-opener.

"I realize we have something of a problem at the Plaza," he intoned solemnly. "High-school kids cruising around, drinking beer, trying to find girlfriends. Makes life difficult sometimes for the folks who go there to do some shopping."

Martin Lasker, junior reporter for the *Millville News*, stared somberly at the slowly rotating heads of his pocket cassette recorder.

This interview was going to be very dull unless the Chief had more to say. From the files back at the office, he knew that the paper ran a story every June on what it called 'the teenage problem' and what was likely to happen with it during the coming summer months. The nearest thing to a teenage problem in Millville was the Pioneer Shopping Plaza out near the highway to Waterbury. It really wasn't much of a problem, but a few people complained regularly and—well, Lasker had to write something. He was new at the paper, as everyone reminded him and it was his first job after college.

"So what I'm going to do," Chief Sturdevent continued ponderously, "is to have a man there every night to keep an eye on things. Make sure the kids move along and don't clutter up the place."

"What about the kids who go there for something, to get a hamburger? Kids that aren't going to cause any trouble."

"That's fine. No sweat. We aren't going to bother them as long as they go about their business, have a good time and don't bother anybody else. We'll be keeping an eye on the ones who haven't got anything better to do with their time and just go to the Plaza to hang out. You get five or six loiterers and then maybe you got a little trouble."

"Chief—"

"Let me also say this, Martin," the Chief added, holding up one hand as if he were still directing traffic. "The great majority, the overwhelming majority, of kids in our town are fine kids and we never have any trouble with them. They're good kids in a good town and we're all happy about that. I think we have a nice relationship with them, a kind of rapport almost, I guess you'd call it. But like any place else we have a few who get into trouble from time to time. Oh, nothing serious, but they can be a nuisance, and that's the situation we have out at the Plaza. Just a few regulars who spoil it for everybody else, drag-racing in the parking lot and what have you."

Sturdevent lit up a menthol cigarette. He had never been interviewed by the local paper before—or by anyone outside of the Department, for that matter—and the idea had originally appealed to him. Now it seemed like just another thing. Why did they send practically the newest, lowest member of their staff?

"We've had letters from some parents saying that the kids who cause trouble at the Plaza are from out of town—Waterbury, Torrington, Naugatuck. What do you think of that?"

"Well… maybe there are some out-of-towners involved, but I doubt it. Kids move in groups, they like to be where their friends are. Over to Waterbury now, they got three or four big shopping plazas of their own, and I know for a fact that they have a much bigger problem with the kids hanging out there than we do here. Anyhow, as I said, we'll be keeping a close watch on the situation and we'll be checking drivers' licenses and so on. We'll soon find out who's who." Sturdevent stood up and stretched. "It's a hot one today. Is that all?"

Lasker wasn't quite through, but he could see that the Chief wanted to leave now, so he switched off his cassette. "Yes, I think that'll do, but I may come back to you tomorrow for a few more quotes, if I may."

"No problem." The Chief smiled broadly. "I hate to run, Martin, but I promised my boy I'd hit some flies to him tonight You know, Sunday is opening day of the Little League and he's trying to get as much practice in as he can."

"Oh, I know," Lasker replied. "I'll be there myself."

"Good, are you covering it for the *News*?"

"That's right"

"My boy is number eleven on the Giants. Plays shortstop."

"I'll watch for him."

The two men now stood in the front lobby of the police station.

"Well you're going to be quite an all-round reporter, if you cover everything from police news to sports."

Lasker didn't like the patronizing tone in the Chiefs voice but he smiled politely. "Thanks again, Chief Sturdevent."

"My pleasure, son."

As Martin Lasker turned to leave, the front door flew open and banged against the wall as a tall, thin, red-faced man wearing blue coveralls and a dirty tee-shirt rushed in, bumping the reporter out of his way.

"Chief Sturdevent?"

"Yes?"

"Can you come out to my place right away? Something terrible has happened. Somebody—"

"Hold on, hold on." Sturdevent held up his stop-sign hand again. "Who are you? Don't I know you?"

"Name's Cy Bondarevsky. I have a farm out on—"

"Jersey Road," the Chief finished the sentence for the farmer. "I bought some of your sweetcorn last year. Mighty good it was, too."

The scene was growing stranger and stranger for Martin Lasker. Bondarevsky was obviously very upset and sweat flowed from his face. Sturdevent, on the other hand, was a veritable lagoon of placidity.

"Somebody's butchered one of my best cows," the elderly man moaned loudly. "Butchered her to pieces. You got to come out and take a look. I want the ones who did it caught."

Lasker's eyes widened. This could be news.

"Hold on, now," Sturdevent murmured quietly. "Just tell me what happened. Exactly."

"I just told you," the farmer shot back quickly, anger colorings his distress. They hacked her up. I come straight in here to get a policeman."

"Why didn't you phone up?" Lasker asked. Both Bondarevsky and Chief Sturdevent looked at him sharply: the Chief with annoyance for the interruption, and the farmer with sheer incredulity, as if Lasker were insane.

"I come right in here, I didn't hang around. I was just in from the lower pasture and how was I to know but those nuts might still be around the farm somewhere? I wasn't taking no chances. Are you a detective?"

"No, I'm Martin Lasker, of the *Millville News*."

"Oh." Bondarevsky turned back to the Chief. "Are you coming? My help's gone home for the day and I'm alone there."

"All right, I'm coming," Sturdevent replied unhappily. "You're only about ten minutes down Jersey Road, aren't you?" he asked still hoping to get away quickly.

"That's right, foller me, my car's out front."

"Okay." Bondarevsky turned and went out the front door.

"Chief."

"Yeah?" Sturdevent started walking away to the back of the station.

"Mind if I ride along with you? I'd like to see this myself."

"Suit yourself," Sturdevent called back. "But I'm not driving you back here. I'm going home after this, and that's over near Dayton's Brook."

"Okay, I'll walk from there." Lasker hurried after the portly policeman.

"I suppose you're the agriculture correspondent for the paper too," Sturdevent said as they got into the police car.

"I don't think we have an agriculture correspondent," Lasker replied with a chuckle. "And I don't know much about farms."

"Neither do I. There's our man."

Sturdevent had pulled around to the front of the station house. Bondarevsky leaned out the window of a battered old station-wagon and waved. Then he drove off with the police car right behind. It was supper time in Millville and there weren't many vehicles on the roads.

"This sounds unusual," Lasker offered after a few moments of silence. "Ever heard of anything like this happening before?"

"Hell, no. The worst kind of thing happens here is a brawl down to Gino's Bar every now and again. Or somebody borrowing somebody else's car for a joyride. If you want to be a crime reporter you sure picked a bad place to get a start, son."

"I don't particularly want to be a crime reporter. What do you think of that guy's story?"

"We'll see when we get there. I expect he's too upset to make real sense. Cows cost quite a bit these days."

"It's hard to be mistaken about a butchering."

"Maybe. And then again, maybe one of the hands left some hunk of farm machinery running and that cow just walked into it. Cows are dumb animals, I do know that much."

"What do you know about this guy Bondarevsky?"

"Not much. His family used to own quite a bit of land. He still has a good-sized farm but he's been selling it off piece by piece lately. Too much for him, I guess."

"Who's he selling to?"

"People slinging up raised ranch houses. And one group of New York boys are planning to put up a complex of apartment houses. You know, like the Heritage House Apartments."

"Yeah," Lasker said.

"It'll make quite a change."

"I guess so."

They drove out past School Street, which marked the northern limit of the town's residential neighborhoods, and swung onto the old Springfield Road, a back-country turnpike dating from colonial times. Jersey Road was a right turn-off a couple of miles further along.

"He's travelling at a fair pace," Sturdevent said. "I'd give him a ticket for it, but it wouldn't hardly seem fair."

Lasker smiled but said nothing.

"You from Millville originally, Martin?"

"Yes, I am."

"What's your father do?"

"Works out at the Gunntown factory. Getting ready to retire."

"Gunntown. Makes bullets?"

"That's right."

"I guess that's the place that made this town. The rest of the business is pretty small stuff by comparison."

"Yeah."

"I guess most of this area used to be called Gunntown back in the real early days before they got around to incorporating legal townships and so on. There's a Gunntown cemetery over near Naugatuck, at least that's what they call it." Sturdevent paused and then added, "My wife reads a lot about early New England history."

"This looks like the place," Lasker said, leaning forward in the front seat. Bondarevsky had driven into the yard of a ramshackle farmhouse. A heavily dented pickup truck stood nearby. The lawn was badly rutted and dug up from being used as a parking lot. Sturdevent pulled the police car in alongside the farmer.

"House needs a good paint job," the Chief muttered to Lasker as he braked to a stop.

"This way, this way," Bondarevsky shouted, walking quickly backwards away from Sturdevent and Lasker.

"He's still very upset," the reporter commented.

"He sure is. I didn't smell any drink off him back at the station."

"Neither did I."

"We're coming," Sturdevent hollered to the farmer.

They followed Bondarevsky around the side of the house to a grey, weather-beaten barn that had a garage tacked on to the near side. A few chickens strutted around nervously. As they passed the garage Lasker noticed that it was full of farm equipment, some old and rusty, some new, sacks of seed and fertilizer and various other items. That explains why Bondarevsky parks out front, Lasker thought.

"Around here," the farmer called.

"Cowshit," Lasker thought he heard Chief Sturdevent mutter.

A small shed sagged against the far side of the barn. As soon as they turned the corner to face it the policeman and the reporter noticed the smell—heavy, dose and foul. Bondarevsky stood at the door of the shed, pointing inside.

"Why was the cow out here?" Sturdevent asked, his face wrinkled and his voice hollow from trying not to use his nose.

"She was due to calve soon," the farmer replied, "and I could tell she wasn't happy in with the others, so I moved her in here."

Sturdevent grunted and stepped into the shed. Lasker followed dose behind, and Bondarevsky lingered at the door. A single light-bulb at the end of an extension cord dangled from the low ceiling. The air was very hot and the stench was almost unbearable. Flies buzzed thickly.

"Jesus Christ," the Chief said.

Martin Lasker felt his throat seizing up.

"I told you it was horrible," Bondarevsky whined in the background. He sounded sad and self-pitying, but calmer now that he had witnesses to the disaster that had befallen him.

Lasker leaned back against the thin board wall of the shed and closed his eyes. He felt sick and dizzy, and he was sweating freely. Sturdevent took another tentative step forward into the shed and stopped. He didn't know what to do.

"I don't get it," the Chief said finally.

Lasker opened his eyes. He tried breathing through his mouth but the smell was inescapable and there was an ugly taste to the air.

The dirt floor of the shed had been covered with a layer of hay, which was now heavily splattered with blood. Bondarevsky's cow — most of it — was in one corner. The head and two forelegs lay about three feet away from the fat, mutilated torso. One of the hind legs stretched out away from the body at an unnatural angle. Lasker thought it stretched very far. The other hind leg was not in sight, presumably hidden beneath the body. Now Lasker saw that there was blood everywhere, blood and tufts of coarse hair. Bondarevsky was still whining in the doorway but neither Sturdevent nor Lasker took any notice of him.

"This animal wasn't cut up," the Chief suddenly said, and the calm, ordinary tone of his voice startled the reporter. "This animal was *not* cut up." Sturdevent had been studying the cow's head and he now stepped gingerly over to the torso.

Bondarevsky fell silent.

"What do you mean?" Lasker asked.

"Well look here. This leg looks as if it was pulled right out of its socket. The hide is stretched and part torn away, but it doesn't look like it was cut with a knife. Same goes for the head — like it was yanked right off."

Lasker took one step forward and peered down at the dismembered animal. The blood and flies were too much. He couldn't tell if Sturdevent was right. It didn't make sense.

"Look at the way the blood splattered," Sturdevent continued. It looks like about eight strong guys came in here and tore this cow to pieces with their bare hands. Or else — "

"Or else what?" Bondarevsky spoke up.

"Or else the cow exploded. All by itself."

"Cows don't explode," Lasker said.

"You don't know for sure."

"He's right," Bondarevsky said. "Cows don't explode. I've been a farmer all my life and I never heard of such a thing. That cow was hacked up by somebody with a sick, sick mind."

"Well, I don't know," Sturdevent sighed. "But it doesn't look like a cut-up job to me. Look here along the belly." The cow's underside was split open and part of the fetus had slid out, in a congealing pool of blood and entrails. "The calf isn't cut, the organs aren't cut, the cow's skin has this jagged tear from the throat to the ass. Get an animal doctor in if you want to, I'm not going to start mucking around with this mess, but it doesn't look like knife-work to me. That's all I'm saying." He stood up and wiped his hands on his trousers. "Christ, what a sight. I'm getting out of here."

Sturdevent hopped across the scattered remains of Bondarevsky's cow and stepped out of the shed. Lasker followed quickly, glad to leave.

"What are you going to do?" Bondarevsky asked.

Sturdevent was patting perspiration off his face with a folded handkerchief. "Tonight, nothing. Tomorrow morning I want you to send your field hands in to see me. Maybe one of them knows something."

"Aren't you going to do anything now?"

"I told you, it doesn't look like a crime to me. It looks strange, I'll say that. But I can't send the coroner out on this kind of job, and we don't have a vet on the town payroll. If you want to pay for it I'd suggest you get a vet out here to give you his opinion. The state and county agriculture offices will all be closed now anyway, but we'll give them a call in the morning and see what they can do."

"I don't know... I pay taxes... what for? ...it's too late for a vet now..." the farmer moaned on, mostly to himself, walking around in small half-circles, his hands hanging uselessly by his sides.

"I'll take a look around the back and in the barn," Sturdevent said to Lasker. "You wait here with Mr. Bondarevsky. Ask him anything you can think of." The Chief shrugged and walked away. When his back was turned to the young reporter he smiled briefly to himself. It was a gruesome, sickening business, but for Sturdevent the whole thing was offset by Bondarevsky's perpetual cry-baby act. Sturdevent thought farmers were supposed to be a tough, hardy band, unafraid of a little blood and dirt. Well, there was a lot of blood here, but he had had it with the old man. The police chief was more interested in exactly what had happened to the cow. He was sure it hadn't been carved, though he realized he could be wrong. He was no expert in knife-work, but he had seen enough of it to recognize certain signs. The tears looked wrong, and the undamaged entrails. No puncture marks. No signs that the cow had been killed quickly first—such as a bashed-in skull. Who would try to dismember a live and struggling cow? And the hind leg, torn and stretched from its joint, but the skin not completely broken. It was a puzzle, all right. Cows didn't explode.

Sturdevent pushed the tall grass behind the barn around with his foot. He didn't have the slightest idea of what he should be looking for.

Martin Lasker decided that a few quiet, straightforward questions might help soothe the farmer somewhat.

"Have you noticed anything unusual around here lately?"

"Nothing. Just the same as always, until today."

"Do you know of anyone who might want to do this kind of thing to you, Mr. Bondarevsky?"

"No, I don't know. We're all friends out here. Who would do something like this? A sick, sick person. I don't know any sick persons. Someone from the city maybe."

"But why would someone come all the way out from the city to kill a cow?"

"Sick, I tell you, sick."

"Have you seen any strangers around here lately?"

"Nobody… I don't know. That's a road out there. Cars go by. Maybe somebody. I don't pay any attention." Bondarevsky looked profoundly unhappy. He wanted someone arrested immediately.

"Well, you're sure you haven't noticed anything strange or unusual around the farm lately?"

"Like what thing?"

"I don't know," Lasker replied helplessly. "Anything that struck you as out of the ordinary. Anything at all."

"Only that the swamp-fire was back."

"What's that?" Lasker asked, although he had an idea to what the farmer was referring.

"The swamp down the bottom of Hollow Road. It lights up sometimes at night. Phosphorescence from the swamp gas."

"Oh yeah? But is that unusual?"

"I saw it about two weeks back. First time since 1955. Probably been there every year in between, but a couple of weeks back was the first time I saw it since. Had a lot of it back then. I only saw it once this time. From the loft in the barn. It looks pretty, sort of."

Bondarevsky was now a bit calmer and Lasker was pleased that it was going well. "Anything else besides the swamp-fire?" Where was Sturdevent?

"Not enough rain. We can use some more rain."

"Uh-hunh."

"Usually June's all right for rain. July's worse, but June's usually all right."

"Everything seems okay," Sturdevent hollered from the barn doorway. "You coming, Martin?"

"Right, Chief. Are you okay?" Lasker asked the farmer.

"Okay. Goodbye," Bondarevsky replied flatly and turned to the shed. Now he stepped unhesitatingly inside.

Lasker stood several yards away for a few moments. He thought he could hear the farmer talking to himself. A cool breeze in the gathering dusk carried away most of the grisly smell. The police car honked in the distance and Martin suddenly broke into a run. He didn't want to be left out at this place.

"Maybe it was a knife job," Sturdevent said before Lasker had closed the car door. "I could be wrong, could be wrong about the old man, too."

The car roared down the bumpy country road. The Chief was in a hurry to get home.

"What do you mean? Did you find something?"

"Two jugs of gin in the milk cooler."

"But the old man wouldn't have had time to do a job like that on the cow, clean himself up and come into town. The hired help would be around. Besides, he's too old."

"Maybe, maybe not. He seemed spry enough to me."

"Well, it doesn't tie up with the way he was carrying on. For a while there I thought he was going to break down completely."

"Yeah," Sturdevent said disgustedly. "But that was a bit much, if you ask me. An old geezer like that, he shouldn't be acting like a kid who's dropped his ice-cream in the sand."

"What do you think then?"

"I don't know how to figure it at all I don't see how it could be done. It doesn't look like a knife job but what else could it be? He say anything to you?"

"Only that it's a dry June."

"Shit"

They drove the rest of the way in silence.

The next morning, Lasker spent two hours playing back the tape of his interview with Chief Sturdevent, editing it and trying to cast it into some kind of workable shape. He cut out several large passages where he thought the Chief was simply playing the good PR man, and then a few more sections that struck him as thinly-veiled politics. Then he realized he had very little left with which to work, so he started over again. If Sturdevent didn't mind coming across as a blowhard, why should he, Lasker, worry about it?

After an hour or so the whole project seemed terribly dull to him. He left the office and walked down the street to Mike's Coffee Shop.

Sitting at the counter, idly stirring the muddy liquid, he wondered if he should write an article, a news story, on Bondarevsky's cow. It was news, at least by Millville standards, but what to say about it? One of farmer Cy Bondarevsky's cows died a mysterious death late yesterday afternoon... Or: Ritual cow murder? ...Or: Local cow blows up? No handle on this story either. It was a bad, hot week. Get more facts, some facts, any facts.

Back at the office he telephoned the police station and, after a brief pause, was switched through to Chief Sturdevent.

"Yes, Martin?"

"Did you talk to Bondarevsky's hired help this morning?"

"Sure did. They were in here waiting when I arrived. The two Denny brothers and Manny somebody-or-other, I got his name here on a piece of paper somewhere. Portuguese kid. Nice enough."

"What's their story?"

"They help out the old man three days a week, Tuesday, Thursday and Friday. Start early and go home early. They didn't see or hear anything unusual yesterday."

"Why didn't they stick around until the old man got back from the other pasture?"

"They knock off at four sharp, whether Bondarevsky is around the barn or out in the fields. I called him and he confirms it. Nothing unusual."

"Do you believe them?"

"They looked mighty scared to me, son. What's in that shed isn't a pretty sight at any time of the day, and especially not first thing in the morning."

"So that leaves you—?"

"Nothing. I'm trying to get a vet from the county to go out to the farm this afternoon and see what he makes of it. Otherwise it's closed for good. That mess is rotting fast and Bondarevsky wants to bury it now, but I asked him to hold off till noon. I should know by then whether or not anybody's coming."

"Uh-hunh. I'll check back with you then too."

"Suit yourself."

"Thanks, Chief."

"By the way."

"Yes?"

"I did come up with one theory."

"What's that?"

"Suppose the cow moseyed around inside that garage full of junk and swallowed a small gas cylinder. I saw a couple of them out there and that kind of thing can happen. They've fished stranger things out of animals."

"Yes."

"If she did swallow a gas cylinder—"

"Then it could explode...?"

"Exactly."

"Want me to print that theory in the newspaper?"

"Hell, no!"

CHAPTER TWO

High on West Side Hill, overlooking the Waramaug River which flowed through the center of Millville, was the R. W. Emerson Elementary School, a squat, dun-colored breadbox of a building that had been constructed a few years after World War II. It had four hundred students, twenty-one teachers and the usual contingent of additional staff ranging from principal to nurse to janitor. The school grounds included a play-yard, a basketball court, a lumpy football field that sloped at an awkward angle and a parking lot. In the school's entrance foyer was a bust, which had been a gift from Millville High School's Wood & Metal Works class of 1949. This pasty-faced creation bore the legend: R. W. Emerson (1803-1882).

At the other end of the building, just outside the rear exit, Joey Pomar waited for his sister, Maria. Why was she always last? Not one of the last kids to leave school every day, but *the* last. Joey marched back and forth by the door, kicking the cement walk, the overhang of crab grass, a pebble, sighing loudly at least four times a minute. She would come as always, in her own good time.

Joey was ten, just turned, and Maria was seven. He had to take her home from school every day before he could go off and play until supper-time. Why was she so pokey? Ladylike and proper, his mother had told him on more than one occasion, when he had complained. But to Joey that just meant stupid. Of course, Maria was cute, and Joey loved her, but she was a nuisance at times. He always felt he was walking in a slow procession when they made their way home.

"Where you been?" Joey asked the ritualistic useless question as Maria finally appeared.

"Getting my books together," she answered simply.

"It doesn't take that long to get your books together." the boy said as they walked along.

"I had to put my pencils in my pencil-box and straighten up the papers in my desk and everything." She spoke sweetly and patiently. It was a carbon copy of many previous conversations that they had had on the way home.

"That's stupid," Joey muttered. He just threw his pencils and papers and ruler and anything else he had been using into the desk any which way. That's what a school desk was for.

They came to the path at the beginning of the long, hilly tract of scrub brush and woods that took up where the football field left off. It had been used by students for years as a shortcut to the Meadow Street-Palmer Road neighborhood in which the Pomar family lived. The land was largely undevelopable—too rocky and irregular—but it was a favorite place for schoolboy games and exploration. It had a small stream, and in the summer Joey and his friends would turn over rocks at its edge looking for salamanders. Length and a gold band down the back were the prized features. Joey wished the stream was large enough for fish, but half the time it was dried up altogether and wasn't any use.

Not far away from the stream was a stagnant old well. At least, the children called it a well, but it was actually more of a small frog pond, about eight feet across. For the last couple of years there hadn't been any tadpoles or frogs; just a few rusty beer cans and weeds. "Nothing," Joey said as they skirted the well.

They came clear of a clump of trees and started up the next hillock. At the top the tall grass gave way to a large rock formation, which was the best site in the area for the boys' army games. The rocks and boulders provided many natural pockets and passageways, making it an ideal place to attack or defend. The south face was a sheer drop of nearly twenty feet—a giant cliff to Joey.

"Come on, come on," Joey shouted as he hopped from rock to rock. He liked the spot. You could see Palmer Road below, about a half mile in the distance. The cars and houses looked very small, like toy models.

"Be careful, Joey, and wait up," Maria called to her brother as she slowly, methodically, negotiated each step of the route.

Joey came to the edge of the cliff. He would stretch out flat on his belly and peer over the edge, while Maria caught up with him. He often got down on the ground here and stared. It made him nervous but excited him too. Maria would never come within ten feet of the edge, but it didn't frighten him. He wondered if it would be horribly painful to fall, or if you'd black out before hitting the ground at the bottom. Joey wondered if blacking out was exactly the same as falling asleep. Sometimes he thought he'd like to be an ant for a while. They could go off the edge and float all the way down without getting hurt. They were small enough. Sometimes he flicked roaming ants over the edge with his finger and tried to imagine the slow descent.

The bottom was dull: a small, flat clearing before the woods began again. Usually there was junk at the base of the cliff. Teenagers left beer cans, bottles, paper bags and dozens of cigarette butts. Once Joey and a friend had found a woman's panties. They couldn't imagine why someone would leave her panties in such a place.

Today when he looked over the edge Joey saw a vibrant blue light reaching almost halfway up the stone face. A cold wind hit him, sending his hair straight up into the air, and he jumped back involuntarily. *What was that?* Joey peered over the edge again, just enough so that he could see. It was a blue light, roughly oval-shaped, and it shimmered brilliantly. The jet of cold air was steady but silent.

Was it a kind of fire, he wondered? No, there was no heat, no smoke—although the blue color reminded him of flames. Maybe it was some kind of gas cloud. No, that couldn't be right; the wind would blow it all away, and although this thing moved strangely it stayed in the same place. What could it be? Joey stared with wonder. He realized he wasn't at all afraid of it, and he was proud of himself. There was nothing to be afraid of. He didn't know what it was, but it didn't seem harmful or dangerous. This was pretty. It was always changing, moving, flickering, glowing. It was more than pretty, he decided, it was beautiful.

"Come on Joey," Maria called from several yards behind the boy.

"Come here."

"Let's go home."

"Come here and look at this." Joey did not want to leave now. He had never seen anything like this before.

"Look at what?"

"There's something down here."

"What?"

"I don't know. Come on and take a look." Without looking back over his shoulder he waved to his sister to join him.

"I don't want to look. I want to go home."

"This is fantastic, Maria. Come here."

"*Joey*, come on."

"Just take a peek. I promise, you never saw anything like this before."

Maria edged a few inches forward and stopped. She didn't like these rocks and she didn't like heights, and she was not going to get down on the dirty ground to look at some dumb thing with Joey.

"Jo-*eey*. Let's go home," she insisted. "I don't want to look down there. You could fall, and then what? Come on, please. I'll walk faster," she said with sudden inspiration. That should please him.

"Just a second." Joey continued to gaze at the incredible apparition before him. Maria had to see this, somebody had to see it. He wished that some of his friends would come by so they could see it too. Maria was just a baby, and a girl, but she was at least better than no other witness at all. Joey scrambled to his feet and ran back to where his sister stood.

"Come on." He grabbed her hand.

"Where are we going? Don't go so fast," Maria protested as Joey hurried her across the far side of the stony rise and into the tall grass.

"I want to show this to you. It'll only take a minute."

"What is it?"

"Some kind of light down here."

They came to the path which skirted the stone face and Joey slowed his pace abruptly. Better to be careful. After all, he didn't know what this thing was and he had Maria with him. Down here on the ground with it, it might be... Joey stopped before the next bend in the rock, which he knew turned into the small clearing where the thing was. Maybe it wouldn't be there now.

"Stay here," he whispered to his sister, but she would not release his hand.

"I don't want to wait here, I want to stay with you." She spoke in her normal voice, which annoyed Joey. She held on to his fingers tightly. "I want to go home."

"Okay, okay," the boy said, ignoring her last remark. "But stay behind me." He put his school bag on the ground, took a deep breath and stepped forward into the bend of the path.

And stopped.

The dazzling rich blue light embraced them where they stood. The wind whirrushed around their ears, but it wasn't exactly a wind either. Invisible, fast, cool, it was like a wind, a silent, invisible streaming movement. The light danced and shivered in a breath-taking display of changes, never still, never the same. It grew from the ground almost to the top of the stone face, where Joey had been a few minutes before. It was hypnotic and hopelessly beautiful. It was blue, and yet it seemed to be all colors, the only color. The wild foliage growing at the rim of the clearing, normally a crisp green in June, seemed drab and lifeless, an undergrowth of khaki.

Joey was paralyzed with fear and uncertainty. His muscles were rigid with tension and he held Maria's hand very tightly. This was incredible, this was something he had never heard of before, and he thought it must be something no one had ever heard of.

What was that? Did he hear something? Not the sound of wind, nor of leaves rustling, but something far different, far stranger than anything he knew. It sounded like voices, tiny voices, speaking from a great distance, like a conversation, conducted in some foreign language that drifted up from the bottom of a very deep cave. Joey thought, this can't be.

Maria worked her hand free from his and knelt on the ground. She brought her hands together, as in prayer, and stared into the blue light.

How long had they been there?

"Come on," Joey said, surprised at how weak and muffled his own voice sounded. Maria didn't respond at all. What was he afraid of? Was this thing dangerous? It didn't seem so. It was just so remarkable, he didn't know what to do. What was Maria doing?

"Maria, come on."

"Kneel down, Joey."

"What?" He could hardly hear her voice.

"Kneel down."

Joey got down beside her on one knee. "What are you doing?"

"Look." Her eyes were alive with the fire.

1 don't know what it is."

"Look."

"I see it."

"Look," she said, never moving her eyes from the light. "At the center."

Joey squinted at the brilliance. It was so much change and interplay he couldn't make out anything in particular. Shapes forming, melting, blending, re-forming. You could see so much, or nothing but deep blue light.

"What is it?" Joey asked.

"Her."

"What?"

"Our Lady. The Virgin Mary."

Joey suddenly began to shake. It couldn't be, but Maria sounded so absolutely sure of herself. And it was the one explanation Joey hadn't thought of.

"No," he said, weakly.

"It is, Joey, it is. Look." Maria's face seemed to radiate joy.

Again he looked. Could it be? The sounds he thought he heard, the wind-like movement rippling over his body, that miraculous light… He felt small, helpless and alone in his confusion. The Virgin Mary. It had happened, he knew. She had appeared at Fatima and Lourdes, and other places, but they were all very far away and years ago. This was Millville, now.

"Yes," Maria said clearly.

Joey looked at his sister. Her face was bathed in the glow of the light and her wide-open eyes continued to shine brightly. He turned back to the apparition. Was that a woman's face in the center, he wondered? It could be… anything. But sometimes it did resemble a face, or a body, but somehow unusual or different. Then he thought, there's no reason why She should look like the statues in church, or the pictures on Christmas cards. Nobody really knew what Our Lady looked like.

The fiery blue light belled over them and the sounds seemed much stronger now, though no more distant than before. The wind-movement was faster, cooler and harder, and Joey became more frightened. It was like thousands of invisible fingers now, running all over his body, pinching, feeling, kneading, rubbing in a terrifying cascade. He thought he moaned to Maria to leave, but he wasn't sure. He felt dizzy and cold and he ached all over.

Maria bent over and lay down with her face to the ground. Joey could see her gaily-printed light summer dress swarming and billowing with the same movement as he felt on himself. And her arms and legs—the flesh twisted and rolled and arched as if it were a teeming, living thing unto itself. As if a million tiny fingers had her in their grasp. He knew he looked the same way, he felt it, and he wanted to get out, *out*, OUT of there.

"Maria!"

He fell down beside his sister and pressed his face into the dry earth to hide. The swarm of fingers continued to crawl all over his body. His stomach was so tight it hurt and he gasped, then sobbed. Finally he began to cry in great, jagged bursts. His eyes were shut but the blue light filled them and there was no darkness. The droning sound of voices was everywhere. He wondered if this was a miracle, if he was in the presence of the Virgin Mary, or if he was dying a horrible death. He wanted to reach for his sister but the only movement he was capable of was convulsive crying. He felt flattened into the earth, his body filled with the sounds and light inside, covered with the nauseating creeping-crawling thing outside. Inside—yes, he thought with terror, the noise and light is inside me, lighting my bones, inside my head.

He thought his brain was burning.

———

After several unhappy attempts to write a short piece on the mysterious death of Cy Bondarevsky's cow, Martin Lasker gave up. He discussed the facts of the matter with his editor, Fred Phipps, who agreed to let it go. Like his junior reporter, Phipps found the idea vaguely tantalizing, but the death of a cow was not, in and of itself, news, and if there were something unusual or newsworthy about the death, then they had to be able to report what it was. Which they couldn't.

"Animal stories can be good," Phipps explained. "And in the summer they often get picked up by the wire services if there's anything to them."

"Silly season stuff, you mean?" Lasker asked.

"That's right. You've probably seen the kind of thing I mean. Two-headed calves or an impossibly large litter. One paragraph oddities." Phipps ran one hand over his bushy, white, crew-cut hair. Almost time for another trim.

"I don't think Bondarevsky's cow really falls into that category."

"Neither do I. For one thing, it's nasty, rather than merely strange or amusing. Am I right?"

"Yes, it was very nasty," Lasker confirmed.

"Did any vet actually see the animal? The county ag station?"

"No. They were going to try to send someone over but he couldn't get there in time. The remains just decomposed too quickly in the heat. Bondarevsky and his help knocked down the shed, dug a hole next to it and shoveled the mess in."

"Health hazard, I suppose."

"Yeah, that's what he said."

"Well, I don't see what you can say about it if you haven't got some knowledgeable opinion, and you can't really count the police chief in this kind of thing."

"Bondarevsky wants us to say it's the work of maniac or maniacs unknown and at large."

"That just sounds silly to me," Phipps scoffed.

"That's what I think."

"Another thing you have to consider, Martin. If we run a story with no plausible explanation, it might have the effect of inviting pranks and mischief. Nobody wants that, least of all the other farmers in the area."

"Well, something did happen."

Phipps stood up and walked to the window of his office. He was a wiry man in his mid-fifties, scarcely an inch over five feet tall. In the case-room he had to stand on a wooden crate to inspect the final sections of standing type—an unnecessary routine that Phipps insisted on for every edition. It was one of many things Lasker admired in the man.

"Something did happen, agreed," the editor said. "But what? Hold your notes until you get some reasonable theory."

"If ever."

"Yeah, hold it in your 'if ever' file."

———

Marge Calder looked out her kitchen window. It was another hot afternoon. Too hot to do anything except sit in the sun. Not a cloud in sight. She wore snug white shorts and a blouse that tied up just under her breasts. It was very quiet outside.

A metal lid clattered against a trash can. That would be Sylvia Berkowitz, from the next house. Marge walked outdoors and across the back lawn to chat with her neighbor.

Sylvia was wiping her hands on the apron she wore. Garbage was such a bother. Unsanitary. Nixon, the family dog, a feeble old Alsatian lying in the sun, rolled his head over and looked longingly at the trash can.

"You leave this trash alone," Sylvia said to the dog. He blinked and looked to one side, as if anxious to avoid her accusing stare. There's nothing the matter with your dog food, it's expensive enough. I don't know why you prefer garbage." Nixon was a nuisance, always hanging around trash cans, knocking them over and rummaging through the contents. Personally, she would get rid of him, but the kids would never stand for it. They thought the old dog was funny.

"Hi, Sylvia," Marge Calder said as she approached. "How are you?"

"Hi, Marge," Sylvia replied. "I'm fine but hot." A fine thing. She probably saw me talking to that damn dog again. She'll think I'm batty. Milton just had to get a garbage disposal unit for the kitchen.

"Yes, it's hot enough, that's for sure."

"I think I'll just lie down for a while."

"Stu and I were supposed to go play tennis this evening but I've called up and cancelled. The heat and humidity are just too much."

"I know what you mean," Sylvia said. "Stick to the cool shade."

"I don't mind the sun so much. I'm getting a good tan now." Marge inspected her arms, legs and bare midriff. "But anything strenuous is just silly in this weather."

Sylvia thought she would go inside and make a tall cold drink. Alone. Marge wasn't her favorite company. Something in the distance caught her eye and she tried to focus on it. A mile or two away, was it? In the air.

Marge noticed the distracted look on her neighbor's face and tried to follow the line of Sylvia's vision. In a few seconds she too spotted the unusual sight.

"What do you think it is?" Marge asked. She raised one hand to her eyebrows and peered intently.

"I don't know."

They were looking at a bright blue disc hovering over the treetops more than a mile away. It seemed to flicker, and it was remarkably bright for broad daylight. It stayed in the same place, neither rising, falling or drifting.

"Do you believe in flying saucers?" Marge asked after a few moments.

"I don't think so, no," Sylvia said with a chuckle she didn't even try to repress.

"I've never seen one, but I suppose they could exist. Don't you think it's possible?"

"Not unless they land on the White House lawn. Then I'll believe it."

"What do you think that is then?"

"Probably just a big kite or a balloon, dear. I wouldn't worry about it too much."

Marge continued to stare into the distance.

CHAPTER THREE

Joe Garfield sat on his front porch sipping cold Ringnes Special beer from the bottle, as he did almost every night in the summer. It was nearly ten o'clock, early yet. Sometimes he sat until one or two in the morning if it was a nice night and the fireflies were out. He would go through twelve or fourteen bottles of the Norwegian beer in a good sitting. It was the only beer to drink, the others were dishwater. Joe never got too drunk, but he always ended up feeling fine, and occasionally uttered a few remarks aloud to himself or a passing car.

He was sixty-one years old last month and lately he had given some thought to retirement. He would be eligible next year, and the idea was tempting. He had worked at Gunntown Arms for forty-two years now, without a break. He had started as a short, scrawny kid hauling cases on the shipping dock. Now he was still short but a good deal heavier, bald and still on the dock, though he had been named freight manager eleven years ago. He told the kids what to do. It wasn't a bad job as jobs go, and he seriously wondered if he should retire the minute he was eligible. Some fellows retired and six months later they stopped breathing. He had known one or two like that. Maybe he should stick with the job. I'm too old to get interested in gardening or anything like that, and too young to sit around watching quiz shows on TV all day. Have to do something.

Across the street, and two houses down, a television set blared loudly. Those damn Italians always have that thing on full blast. In another half hour they'll start arguing about the late movie again—that happened at least twice a week.

Directly across the street the Halsey household was quiet, as ever. Nice, peaceful folks. That's more like it. Some nights Joe could see the faces of the Halsey boys, Bob and Tom, pressed against the screen of their bedroom window. They counted passing cars one taking Fords, the other Chevrolets. Once in a while they'd whisper a sharp 'Hi' to Joe, letting him know they were there instead of sleeping. He ignored them. When he sat down for his evening beer he didn't want to get into a conversation. Especially not with a couple of kids.

Tonight was a good night, a fairly quiet night. Usually there was a lot of coming and going at this spot. Joe's house was next to the corner lot on Barton Street, where it ran into Highland Avenue. But tonight was pleasant and relatively traffic-free. He could hear the soft rustle of a breeze in the sugar-maples on his front lawn. A mere postage stamp of a lawn, but with two fine trees that he loved. Trees kept squirrels and squirrels were essential to a neighborhood as far as Joe was concerned.

Annie Garfield, his wife, came down the hallway to the front door—Joe could hear the pad-pad of her slippers on the linoleum. She stood behind the screen door for a few seconds. "How you doing, Joe?"

"Fine, I'm fine, Annie."

"Do you need another beer?"

"No, I'm still working on this one."

"You're okay?"

"Yeah, I'll come in for another one in a little while. How are you?"

"Okay."

"What are you watching?" He didn't care at all, but whenever she came to the porch he always asked.

"I don't know. Something is on but I'm reading the paper."

"Okay."

"Okay."

After a few more moments Joe heard her moving back into the house. Annie very seldom came out onto the porch and sat with Joe. He liked to sit alone. Early in the evening she might sit for a spell, but when Joe sat down with his beer the porch was his and she left him to it If she'd retire, I'd retire, Joe thought, but she can't. Annie was fifty-eight years old and had a way to go yet before she could afford to quit working. She did the payroll and bookkeeping at the Grand Union supermarket. Annie always was good with numbers, Joe thought.

Joe Garfield happened to be looking squarely at Ernie Pachman's car when it turned bright green and exploded with the most ear-bruising racket he had ever heard.

"Holy shit," he exclaimed, rising to his feet.

The car was parked near the corner of Highland Avenue, diagonally opposite the Garfield house. The corner lot was part of Pachman's yard so Joe had a clear view. The car just seemed to— explode. Suddenly. In a green flash. All four tires blew and the chassis collapsed to the ground as the axles shattered. Glass sprayed in all directions. The hub-caps spiraled into the air, one smashing through a side window in the Pachman house. The headlights and parking lights also blew outwards, like eyes popping out of their sockets. The front bumper ripped loose from one end and twisted in the air, then, tearing loose completely and clanging on the road, bent almost in a circle. The hood peeled back away from the windscreen, letting out dozens of parts and broken chunks of metal from the engine beneath. The steering column heaved up and through the windscreen, and the steering wheel wrenched loose and spun wildly into Barton Street toward the Garfield house. The seats ballooned and then shredded into a storm of upholstery and stuffing, which hung in the air around the car like a woolly cloud. The doors buckled in, then out, and finally snapped onto the ground in pieces. Everything, from the front grille to the exhaust pipe, was chewed up and spat out into the night, all in the space of a few seconds. Most of the debris remained within ten yards of where the car was parked, but the next day one of the door handles was found in Stu and Edie Wright's flower garden, about a hundred and fifty yards down the street. Considering the great force involved, it was extraordinary good fortune that no one was injured.

When the violence and noise ended, Joe Garfield stepped down from his porch and slowly walked towards the car. Ernie Pachman came running out of his house yelling "What the fucking hell is going on?" and other things. A few more people appeared, wives and children standing in their doorways, husbands tucking their shirts in their pants and approaching cautiously.

"Who did this? Who did this?" Ernie Pachman demanded hotly. He was a thin-haired, thin-bodied, nervous insurance agent. He kept picking up destroyed pieces of his car, looking at them for a few seconds and then throwing them aside.

"I saw it Ernie, I saw it," Joe said, striding forward briskly now. "Hang on, I saw it."

Everyone turned quickly to look at him as he moved purposefully through the growing cluster of people. Joe immediately realized the importance of the occasion and he responded to it wholeheartedly.

"You saw it, Joe?" Pachman continued to gesture emptily with his arms. "What the hell happened? Who did this?"

"Nobody did it, Ernie. It just happened."

"Nobody?" Packman was incredulous and angry. He glared at Joe as if he were in fact confronting the guilty party. "Somebody had to do this, it couldn't just happen by itself."

"I tell you, it just happened. I was—"

"Come on, Joe," someone said. "What really happened?"

"I was on my porch," Joe continued, addressing himself to Pachman and ignoring the others. "Your car just suddenly began to fall apart or explode, I guess. There was a kind of green flash." Joe was aware that he was explaining it badly but he couldn't think of anything else to say without sounding even sillier.

"All by itself?" Pachman fairly bellowed. "Fell apart? Exploded?"

"That's right," Joe persevered. It all took place in a couple of seconds. You were out your front door just when it was over. It was very fast and then it was all over."

"I came out when I heard that noise and something came through our window, but it had to have been going on before that, Joe." Pachman's face showed he clearly felt Garfield was holding something back. "These things don't just happen. Somebody had to do it."

"I'm telling you—"

"Either you saw them or you didn't."

"There was a green flash for just a second."

"A green flash?"

"Doesn't look like there was any fire," someone said from the crowd. People began examining the remains with increased attention.

"Not a fire, no," Joe said.

"A green flash?" Pachman repeated blankly.

"The car just flared with it and then—blam!"

"How many beers have you had tonight?" Pachman asked disgustedly and turned away from Joe. "There wasn't any explosion here. No smell of it, no sign of fire." He resumed picking up pieces of his car with a pained look on his face, muttering about vandals and drunks.

Joe Garfield stayed cool and tried to project an air of seriousness and dignity. "Beer has nothing to do with it. The car just went, in nothing flat. One second it was there, and the next—boom!" He put his hands in his pockets and stood his ground calmly. "That's the truth," he added.

Jack Mitchell, a young man of twenty-eight, peered intently at Joe as if waiting for more. "You say it was green?"

"Seemed that way to me. Of course I could be wrong, it all happened so fast, like I said. But it sure looked green to me. Just a big spark, like someone took a picture with a green flashcube. No smoke though, is there? So I guess it wasn't a fire, nor any kind of normal explosion. Damnedest thing."

"Hunh," Mitchell grunted.

"Anybody else see any part of it?" Joe asked the crowd. "Anybody?"

No one spoke up. Many of the people were now milling about restlessly, talking among themselves in small knots.

"I guess not," Joe said to himself. "Just me."

Then the people moved out of the road as a big police car came cruising along. The black-and-white stopped in the middle of the street and a tall, lanky young policeman stepped out slowly, surveying the scene with puzzlement and suspicion,

"What's going on here?" he asked.

Arturo Pomar swung his rattly old Mustang in towards the curb and parked on Water Street, just opposite the studio of RMLV, the local radio station. He checked his watch: it was just after 7.20 p.m. and he was early. He consciously walked slower, but within two minutes he had arrived at the rectory of St Jude's Church. It was a handsome, old redbrick building, flanked by good-sized fir trees. He had passed it hundreds, maybe thousands of times, he thought, but he had never been inside.

The Pomars were good Catholics but they sent their children to Emerson, the public school, because of the simple geographical convenience. St Jude's was on the other side of the river. Besides, the kids went to religion class every Thursday evening. If there were a Catholic school a little closer to home, that would be a different matter; of course they would go.

Pomar pushed the doorbell and heard a brittle ringing from inside the rectory. After a few moments the door opened and an elderly woman smiled at him.

"I've come to see Father Lombardy," he said.

"Yes, come in," the woman answered in high, musical tones. She led him into the first room on the right off the entrance hallway. "Do sit down," she smiled. "Father Lombardy will be down in a minute." She whisked out of the room, leaving the door half-open.

Pomar sat back in a deep easy-chair in front of a large mahogany desk. The Naugahyde squeaked as he made himself comfortable in the chair. He looked around the room. It was obviously the room in which the priest met parishioners on church business. There were three other chairs identical to the one in which Pomar sat, one behind the desk and two arranged at convenient angles in front of it. Pomar wondered idly what they did if they had more than three visitors at the same time. Another room obviously.

There were paintings on the walls—a portrait of Christ wearing the crown of thorns, which was to be expected, another of Christ speaking to a crowd of people, probably the Sermon on the Mount, from the look of it, and on the wall behind the desk, a placid seascape. In a stand-up frame on the bookshelf was a photograph of the Pope. Next to it was a photograph of someone who looked as if he might be a bishop—Pomar couldn't remember who was the bishop of the Hartford diocese. He glanced only briefly at the books in the bookcase; the only title that stood out was *Father Damian*, which, Pomar vaguely recalled, was about a priest who devoted himself to the lepers in Hawaii, or somewhere in the Pacific, a long time ago.

Pomar swallowed and cleared his throat; the priest would be along any minute now. He dreaded this meeting and he felt silly being there. He didn't know any of the priests to talk to, and when he had phoned up they put him on to Father Lombardy, who was polite and said he would be glad to talk to Arturo whenever was mutually convenient. That's what priests were for, among other things. No, it wasn't about a baptism, a wedding, or anything like that. Pomar had a problem. Fine, okay come in as soon as you'd like.

The only thing was, Father Lombardy was one of the younger priests, and Pomar felt awkward about talking to someone in his own age-group about such a personal matter. Well, that's the way it is, he thought; maybe Father Connors or Father Slomcenski, the elder of the four priests stationed at St Jude's, would be even more difficult to talk to. Any way you looked at it, it was a difficult business. Father Lombardy, Pomar knew, left the confessional every twenty minutes to stand on the front steps of the church and have a cigarette. Didn't seem right for a priest.

"Good evening." The priest strode into the room and shook hands with Pomar.

"Father Lombardy, I'm Art Pomar. I haven't met you before, but—"

"How are you?"

"Fine. We go to the eight-thirty Mass and we never seem to have you."

The priest smiled. "No, I usually do the ten or the eleven-fifteen High Mass. It's nice to meet you now, though."

"Yes, Father, thank you." Pomar sat down again.

Father Lombardy went to the chair behind the desk, pulled out the right front drawer, sat back in the chair and propped his feet up, crossed, on the open drawer. He smiled broadly and unwaveringly, like a bright young business executive who had just pulled off an excellent deal.

Pomar felt more awkward than ever. On the very few occasions when Arturo had been to one of Father Lombardy's Masses he had never seen the priest close up, because the Pomars always sat at the back of the church. Now he seemed terribly young, almost boyish. The mass of thick, black, curly hair which reached over the ears, the smile, and the bulk which suggested baby fat rather than muscle or paunch — all combined to give Arturo the feeling that he was about to discuss a very personal matter with someone who was younger than he was. But there was nothing he could do about it now, except carry on and see how it went. The priest lit up a long, thin cigarette.

"How is your family?"

"All right, Father, they're all right."

"You have — is it two children?"

"That's right, Father."

"I've seen them on Thursday nights — right?"

"Yes, Father, that's right."

"They're very attractive children." Father Lombardy's beam reached even further across his face. He seemed to be all teeth and crinkled-up eyes.

"Thank you. Father." Pomar took the priest's remarks at face value and was pleased by them. He was proud of his children.

"Is your family from Millville?"

"No, Father, my family is mostly in Bridgeport and nearby." Pomar sat back in the chair for the first time, happy to talk about anything other than what had brought him to the rectory in the first place. "After high school I worked around a lot of places — here in Connecticut, New York, Massachusetts — all over. But I landed here, got married and been here ever since."

Father Lombardy nodded several times while Pomar spoke. "I see. Like me, a little bit." The priest smiled confidentially. "I've been in four or five parishes already. St Jude's is the longest so far, almost two years now. I'm from Trumbull originally."

"Oh yes." Pomar knew that Trumbull was a wealthy small town somewhere in the direction of New York, but nothing else about the place. He's still so young — why did he leave so many parishes so quickly? Not very popular, maybe too modem. The young priests were always fighting about something or other — growing long hair, holding folk Masses, taking part in demonstrations. Not much scope for that in Millville, but Pomar nursed a worry in the back of his mind that Father Lombardy was of the same breed.

"Now then, Mr.—"

"Call me Art, Father, everybody does."

"Okay, Art, how can I help you?"

Pomar studied the floor. "It's about my children, Father."

"Yes?"

"Well, they're very good children, Father." The priest nodded. "But this last week or so we've had this thing, this kind of problem with them."

"Problems are there to be solved," the priest said with quiet assurance. "Let's hear about it."

"Well, it sounds silly or impossible…"

"Art, there's no need to feel silly about telling me what's what. I hear everything, but everything."

"I know, Father."

"So just relax and let it come out." The priest smiled reflexively now, thinking he was about to hear another case of childhood shoplifting or some such delinquency.

"Well," Pomar plunged in, his eyes widened, still staring at the floor, "my kids came home last Friday and said they saw the Virgin Mary in the woods after school"

"What? The Virgin Mary?" Father Lombardy's smile seemed to stiffen a little.

"That's right, Father," Pomar replied, looking aggrieved and bending his head even lower.

"Well—" the priest started to speak.

"And then they came home on Monday and said the same thing, and Tuesday, and they were quite sure of it, Father." The words came quickly to Pomar now. "And so I called last night and made an appointment to see you, and they came home again today and said they saw Her again, and this time the boy down the street, Philip Rowley, he was with them and he says yes, they saw Her. Father, they are good children and we have never had any kind of trouble with them before. Joey is a little carefree, but no more so than any other boy his age. They are good children, but I don't know what to think."

During Pomar's brief outburst the smile on Father Lombardy's face had shifted into a look of serious concern. Pomar was clearly very upset and, for the first time, the priest understood it. Father Lombardy removed his feet from the desk drawer and leaned forward soberly. Pomar continued staring at the carpet, a worn, lifeless grey pile, casting frequent short glances up at the priest.

"Well, Art," Father Lombardy began, speaking slowly, as if choosing each word as he came to it, "the first thing I would say is that it's important to remember that many, many children, at one time or another during their youth, think they have a vision of some kind—the Virgin Mary, Our Lord, or some favorite saint. It is not at all uncommon, and I say they *think* they have a vision because in virtually all such cases that is exactly what happens: the child imagines the vision, it doesn't actually take place. Something like that happened to me when I was seven or eight, this kind of intense religious experience. It's not unhealthy, in fact it can be quite a good thing, as long as the child is made to understand that the vision or visitation is not real." Lombardy paused but Pomar said nothing, so the priest continued. "As I said, there are a great many cases like this every year, but you yourself know that the number of actual, genuine appearances is very, very, small."

"Lourdes, Fatima," Pomar said quickly, nodding his head.

"That's right, and a few questionable incidents that the Church hasn't approved or disputed—there is a very strong Marianist cult in Garabandal in Spain that Rome has recently denounced, for example. In a few cases there may be room for doubt or uncertainty, and of course it is always possible that the incident is genuine. So where we have many people in the same place reporting a visitation, responsible people, where there is reason to believe that it may be real, then, naturally, the Church will look into it. But, for the most part, cases like this are simply hallucinations or dreams."

"Yes, Father, that is what I think, too." Pomar looked relieved. "But what do I do about Joey and Maria? How do I talk to them about it? They are just children." Pomar worried a loose button on his shirt.

"I understand, and it's not easy. I think you have to be firm with them, but above all, don't be so firm as to discourage their faith as a whole. That is good, and must be nurtured. But you can tell them that they are just ordinary children, like any others they go to school with, and they shouldn't expect that the Virgin Mary would appear to them. That's pride, which was the cause of Lucifer's fall from grace. And you can tell them that if it was Our Lady She would have spoken to them—"

"But they say She has, Father."

"What? She has?"

"Yes, they say so. I forgot to say that earlier."

Father Lombardy looked at the nervous parent across the desk from him for a few seconds. He began to think he had made a mistake by trying to cut this whole matter short with a fast pep talk. Maybe there was more to it.

"Where do your children say they had this visitation, Art?"

"In the woods near Emerson School."

"Yes, I know the place. And what did they say Our Lady looks like?"

"A fire, Father, a burning fire of blue, with Our Lady in the center."

"I see. And She spoke to them? What does She say?"

"Well, nothing, Father, at least nothing sensible, that is, from what they say. All they hear is a voice, or maybe voices, but Joey says you can't hear it too good and you can't understand what it's saying."

"So it's just a noise that the children *think* is the voice of Our Lady?"

"That's right, Father, but they're quite sure of it. I tried to tell them it was probably just the wind or something, but they say no, it's Her."

"I see." That didn't sound so bad, Father Lombardy thought. "What else? How long does She appear to them each time?"

"I guess it differs, Father. The first time, last week, they came home at supper-time, which was hours after they should have been home. Their clothes were all dirty and wrinkled, their faces all dirty and their hair wild. I didn't even listen to them then, I just assumed they had been fooling around in their school clothes and bawled them out, but good. The last couple of days they've been late, but not all that much."

"Mm-hmn. And you say they're quite sure it's Our Lady?"

"Absolutely, Father. That's why I come to see you. They don't listen to anything I say. It's like their own private thing now, neither my wife nor I can break through it to them, and we're worried sick."

"Do they say that She has done anything while they see Her?"

"What do you mean, Father?"

"Well, anything remarkable, like a sign or signal, or something like, well, something miraculous? Is there any suggestion of that?"

"No, they haven't said anything like that. Just that She appears there in a heavenly blue light No, they've said nothing about any miracles."

"I see. No messages, no miracles, just the apparition of Our Lady."

"Yes, Father."

The priest leaned back in his chair again, toying idly with a pencil, as if he were about to write out some spiritual prescription for the Pomar children. Well, Art, it still sounds to me like a fairly typical case of strong faith pushed too far by overactive imaginations. In fact, it doesn't even have the usual frills, such as an important message for mankind from Our Lady, or a miraculous sign. So I don't think there's anything to worry about on that account."

"No, I didn't think so either, Father."

"But it is, as I said earlier, important that the children are handled properly. They have to be guided firmly but gently through this little episode."

"Will you talk to them, Father?"

"If you think it's necessary."

"Yes. Yes, please, Father."

"Yes, I think it's important, too."

On the sidewalk in front of the rectory, they shook hands again, awkwardly, and Father Lombardy watched the anxious parent stride away to his car. Makes a change from the routine, the priest thought to himself. He walked slowly back to the door, noticed that the front lawn needed mowing and made a mental note to remind Mr. Parmentier, the school janitor and caretaker.

In his quiet Hoadley Street apartment, Jim Donner folded his sweaty socks in neat squares, placed them in the laundry hamper and stepped into his clean new slippers. The chess pieces stood ready, as always, and the postal clerk was anxious to settle down to it. The latest issues of *Chess Life and Review* had arrived that morning and there were many games to play through, as well as news and gossip to catch up on. Sitting on the toilet, Donner had already flipped through the magazine and seen that it contained a couple of games by Duncan Suttles, the unpredictable Canadian grandmaster. Donner would enjoy those. A year ago he had seen Suttles in person in a major tournament. Suttles had opened the game with P-QR3, which was almost the craziest move you could begin with, as far as Donner was concerned. Still, the man was a grandmaster and he won many games (including the one Donner witnessed).

Donner switched on the Sony; there was plenty of tape yet to run on that reel. He hummed along to himself as he went into the kitchen for a large tumbler of iced tea. The last couple of nights he had given himself a crash course in the King's Gambit and had exorcised the specter of that obnoxious child from his mind. The best reply to that opening had to be the Falkbeer Counter-Gambit, and Donner had played through every main variation until he had it down pat. Fischer's refutation was too problematical for Donner's taste and besides, that's probably what the kids would have studied. The Falkbeer was solid, offered good chances for a counter-attack and had plenty of historical precedent to support it. Donner was confident he wouldn't be caught off guard by the King's Gambit again. He placed the pleasantly cool glass of amber liquid on his special chess coaster, stamped with a bishop's miter, to the right of the chessboard.

But he never got to sit down.

As Donner reached for his chair the room suddenly flared with blue light, a wind seized him and spun him across the floor. Books and magazines began to fly about, clumping against the walls, shredding into confetti-like swirls. The ceiling light shattered in its fixture and the glass sprayed through the air. Donner felt his right side pierced with broken shards, and when he touched it the pain grew much worse and his hand came away with bright red smears. He tried to stand up but the wind slammed him against a wall. Stunned, he collapsed to the floor. He could see everything in the room dancing about in a blur — the chessboard clattering into a corner and rattling there like some mad automaton, the thirty-two pieces flashing through the air randomly, bouncing off walls, the table hammering, jumping, lurching, the reels of tape all unravelling wildly. The blue light was dazzling, and there was a strong droning noise that filled the room, and Donner's head. He leaned on one elbow and the wind took hold again, slamming him into the onrushing sofa. *Rollers*, he thought, and it was the last conscious word to form in his mind. His face caught the arm of the sofa almost squarely. The cartilage in his nose twisted horribly as his mouth erupted in a fount of blood and broken teeth. He began to scream, but convulsive gagging cut it off. The wind slammed him into the door and he blindly fumbled for the knob to escape. He turned it and pulled, but the door wouldn't open more than a crack, as if dozens of other hands were pushing the door closed at the same time. His back was a crisscross of agony, with hundreds of invisible fingers pushing into it fiercely. The fingers lifted him and Donner whirled across the room. His right knee smashed into the tape recorder, cracking open the cabinet and slashing his pants and leg on electrical components. The hair on his head stood out in every direction and began to rip loose from the scalp. The room bulged with blue light, the wind, and a cacophony of snapping, rending, battering noises.

On the ground floor below in Dom's Apizza, Mrs. Ruggieri, owner, proprietor and landlady for the rest of the building, was the first to hear the racket. But Tony, her cook, and the half-dozen or so customers in the shop all looked up at the ceiling within seconds.

"Mother of God what is that man up to?" Mrs. Ruggieri exclaimed.

"Bombed out," Tony said with a shrug.

"I don't think so," the elderly woman answered. She started for the rear exit. Mr. Donner didn't get drunk, she thought. He never did anything. Quietest man in the world. Neat, fussy, polite, a bit dull, maybe even a bit odd, always sitting in his room, but he never got drunk, and he never, never made noise. She knew he played music on the machine but she hardly ever heard a stray bar of it, it was turned down so low and what with the traffic and all.

But now, such a noise.

She ascended the back porch stairs as quickly as she could. The door to Dormer's apartment was open and Mrs. Ruggieri waddled through the kitchen towards the front room. The door there was closed, but the noise coming from behind it was fearsome now and she backed away a step or two as she thought she saw the woodwork pressing out towards her.

"Tony," she said in a whisper, and then she repeated it as a hoarse cry. "Tony, Tony!" She hastened out of the apartment and back down the stairs.

Tony stood nervously by the back door of the restaurant. "His front windows just blew out," he said. "What's going on up there?"

"I don't know, Tony, it sounds terrible and I couldn't get in the room. Call the police, quickly, quickly."

Dom's Apizza was empty when she and Tony hurried back inside. The customers stood out on the street with a growing crowd of passers-by. Suddenly Mrs. Ruggieri realized that the infernal noise from above had ceased.

"Tony, go watch the door. Don't let that fellow get away." She wrenched the phone from the young fellow's grasp and rushed towards the rear exit again. "Hurry, hurry, I'll call the police."

Tony took up a station at the foot of the back porch stairs, none too happy about it. Donner's door, the only one into or out of the small apartment, remained shut.

CHAPTER FOUR

Al Sturdevent was tying the laces of his bowling shoes at the Valley Lanes on Weston Turnpike when Bernie Jackson, the proprietor, tapped him on the shoulder.

"Call for you, Chief."

"Damn." Sturdevent looked up briefly. "All right, Bernie, I'll be right there."

"Okay." Jackson returned to the front desk.

"Damn," Sturdevent muttered to himself again. He finished tying his shoes and went to the phone. He picked up the receiver but didn't say anything for a few seconds as he watched an attractive young girl in tight white shorts and flimsy tee-shirt enter the front door and stride across the lobby. "Yeah," he spoke into the phone. "Sturdevent here."

"Chief, this is Dave Corwin."

"Yes, Dave."

"I'm at Hoadley Street and we have some trouble here."

"What is it, Dave?" Sturdevent could see his teammates at lane nine. They were getting ready to bowl.

"Fellow here's been killed."

"Killed?"

"That's right, Chief, and it doesn't look right. Not one bit."

Sturdevent sighed. "Is Hanley there? Can't he take care of it?"

"He asked me to phone you, Chief."

"He wants me there?"

"That's right. It's the worst thing I've ever seen, Chief," Corwin added.

"Okay, I'll be along in a few minutes."

"We're on the first floor over Dom's pizza joint. You have to come in through the shop, Chief."

"Right," Sturdevent said curtly and hung up. Damn. Tonight's game was important, too. Sturdevent's team, The Giants, were neck-and-neck with tonight's opponents, Todd Tigers for first place in the league.

"All set, Al?" Greg Hibbard, the team captain, asked as Sturdevent returned to the lane.

"No, I just got a call, Greg, and I'll have to leave right away." He threw his ordinary shoes in his bowling bag and zipped it up unhappily.

"Oh, damn, that's too bad." Hibbard said.

"Got anybody here who can sub for me?"

"I thought I saw Maggie Waters' boy here somewhere. We'll find somebody. Too bad you're going to miss it, though." Hibbard hefted a bowling ball idly in his hands.

"Yeah. You better win."

"Right, Al, see you next week, if not before."

Sturdevent left with a brief wave to his fellow Giants and was soon speeding along the Turnpike into town, wondering why this incident had to happen on his bowling night. He couldn't believe that it was as bad as Corwin had suggested on the phone. Still, Hanley wanted him to come in and see it, and Ned Hanley would never do that unless it were something way out of the ordinary.

Hanley was a take-charge guy with plenty of ambition. If he had any kind of personality, Sturdevent thought, if he knew how to talk with politicians, the town leaders, well, then Hanley might even have my job. But that would never happen. And nobody ever gets murdered in Millville.

Sturdevent spotted the crowd of people standing around outside of Dom's as soon as he turned the corner into Hoadley Street. Patrolman Lawson was trying to shoo the onlookers away and keep traffic moving at the same time. Not an easy task, from the looks of it, Sturdevent thought, as he parked in front of the First City Bank's driveway. He strolled up the sidewalk casually, like any other citizen out for an evening walk.

"Okay, Vinnie?"

"Oh, hi Chief. Yeah, I guess." His tone of voice suggested that things were not okay.

"Corwin and Hanley upstairs?" Sturdevent gestured with his thumb.

"Yes, sir."

"I'll send Dave down to give you a hand in a couple of minutes."

"Thanks." Lawson looked with curiosity at Sturdevent's bowling shoes. "Watch out for the glass, Chief, it's all over the place."

"Uh-hunh." Sturdevent looked around and saw that the patrolman was right. He pushed a few splintered chunks of glass with his toe and looked up at the broken windows on the first floor, before stepping carefully into the pizza restaurant. He found Ned Hanley in the back room with Mrs. Ruggieri, Tony and a few other people he didn't recognize. "Hello, Ned."

"Chief. Thanks for coming. I knew you'd want to see this for yourself." To the other people Hanley said, "Okay, you can go now. We'll get in touch if we need you again."

The customers went out quickly. Mrs. Ruggieri and Tony sat in silence. Hanley led Sturdevent out back and up the wooden stairs.

"What is it, Ned?"

"We've got their stories, Chief, but they aren't much of a help. You'll see what I mean when you see the room."

"Who's the dead party?"

"Guy name of James Donner. Lived alone here, worked at the post office for years. Mrs. Ruggieri says he was always very quiet and polite to her, never any trouble whatsoever."

They had stopped, at Hanley's move, on the landing.

"Where is it?" Sturdevent asked. "In there, right?"

Dave Corwin appeared behind the screen door but said nothing. Sturdevent noticed him as a pale presence at the edge of his vision.

"It's pretty nasty in there, Chief. I just want to let you know ahead of time," Hanley said, and turned to the door.

"Yeah, yeah, let's go," Sturdevent replied brusquely. "Hi, Dave."

"Evening, Chief."

"You don't look too good." Sturdevent smiled, but his attempt to sound humorous had no effect on Corwin.

Ned Hanley's burly frame stood in the hallway of the apartment, one arm extended in a gesture towards the room concerned. You still look like a traffic cop, Sturdevent thought as he approached.

"In here, huh?"

"In here," Hanley nodded.

Everything in the room had been destroyed. Sturdevent had been prepared for a mess, but the damage was even more extensive than he had anticipated. He noticed the wallpaper before he even looked for the body. Long strips of it had been peeled away from the wall and hung limply in tatters.

"Look at that wallpaper," he said, matter-of-factly.

"I noticed," Hanley replied.

"You fellows look through any of this stuff yet?"

"No, sir, the only thing we did was get a new light bulb. I had Dave call you as soon as I got here."

"Good, good." Sturdevent had ventured only a few feet into the room. This is going to take time, he thought.

Dave Corwin edged into the doorway, clearly surprised at the composure the Chief was maintaining. "Have you ever seen anything like this, Chief?"

"Nope," Sturdevent answered calmly. "Dave, would you go downstairs and give Vinnie a hand? Clear those people away if you can and collect as much of that broken glass as possible, and don't smudge it."

"Yes, sir."

"Did either of you call Doc Schmidt?"

"He's out to dinner," Hanley replied. "But they're trying to locate him and get him here straight away."

"Good."

Sturdevent surveyed the scene with mounting anxiety. What had taken place in this room was terrible, monstrous, more so than he cared to admit to himself. He hunched down to look closely at the corpse lying on the floor near the door. It was a bloody, torn heap of flesh and protruding bones. The minute he saw Donner's body Sturdevent thought of Bondarevsky's cow, and the more he examined the remains here the more he was sure the two incidents were related. One side of

Donner's face was visible, and the flesh was ripped from the corner of the lips back across the cheek to the eye socket. Most of his hair had been yanked loose and his head was marked by red spots that resembled miniature divots on a golf course.

Donner's arms seemed unnaturally long and Sturdevent suspected that beneath the blood and the tattered clothing they would find stretched and torn muscles, as had been the case with Bondarevsky's cow. But there's no smell here, he noted mentally.

Several objects were embedded in Donner's back. Sturdevent leaned forward a few more inches to try to identify them. He frowned.

"Okay," Sturdevent said, rising to his feet again, "what's the story as you've got it so far?"

"This guy is regular as clockwork, according to Mrs. Ruggieri, who owns the joint downstairs and also happens to be the landlady. Donner never did a thing out of line. Got up, worked, came home, didn't drink, few friends, quiet as a mouse. A cipher, a nobody. We've got nothing on him at the office but we've put out for state and federal information."

"Okay. What happened tonight?"

"About seven-fifteen everybody downstairs started hearing this terrific racket. The old lady tries to get in, but the door is locked and anyway the noise scares her. While they're calling us the noise stops. They say nobody left this apartment—Tony, the guy who cooks, watched the back porch and that's the only entrance. But they could have missed somebody. I got the impression they were hopping around like a bunch of scared rabbits."

"Did they see anybody come in with Donner earlier?"

"No."

"I see. What about—?"

"Chief?"

"Yes?"

"Before Doc Schmidt or anybody else gets here, I want to show you something."

"What?"

"Take a look at this." Hanley knelt down and pointed with a pencil at some torn sheets of printed paper sprinkled about the floor. "These here."

"What are they?" Sturdevent asked, peering about as if not quite sure what in particular he was supposed to be looking at.

"Look at this one." Hanley tapped lightly on a larger fragment. "It's all in Russian."

"Russian? Is that what this is?"

"Yes, sir, I'm ninety-nine per cent certain."

"Well, what about it?"

"I just wondered about our friend here," Hanley said, pointing to the corpse. "Guy works in the post office. Has a house full of stuff written in Russian. Sounds a little peculiar to me."

"You think he might be some kind of spy?" Sturdevent made no effort to hide his smile.

"All I'm saying is it looks unusual, Chief." Hanley's face had reddened slightly. "Unless you know Russian I'd think about asking the FBI to at least look in on it."

"We'll see."

"I just think that we should be on top of the situation from the start."

"Good, good. Christ, this place has been torn to pieces." Sturdevent stood helplessly, wondering where to begin. The room was awash with blood and debris.

"One person didn't do all this, I can tell you that." Hanley lit a cigarette and tossed the extinguished match out into the hallway. "It had to be several people."

"Why?"

"Just look at it—"

"No, I mean why on earth would anybody do this? Go to all this trouble? I can't see anything that's been left untouched. People kill people all the time, but they seldom go to all this bother for trimmings."

"Do you think the people downstairs could be tied in on this?"

"Who?" Sturdevent looked puzzled.

"The old lady who owns the place and her cook, Tony."

"Weren't they working in the restaurant at the time?"

"Yeah, but…" Hanley wanted prompting.

"But what?"

"They're both Italians."

"Meaning what?"

"I don't know," Hanley said in a tone of voice that made it clear he had very definite ideas.

Sturdevent spoke the word: "Mafia?"

"It's a possibility," Hanley affirmed without hesitation. "We have to look into every possibility."

"Sure, Ned," Sturdevent smirked. "You follow up that angle." Hanley would get lost in a broom closet if I wasn't around to keep an eye on him.

"It could be a band of crazies, doing it for kicks," Hanley said quite seriously, making Sturdevent think again of Bondarevsky's bitter explanation. "Like the Manson gang." Sturdevent didn't respond to this line of theory. "Hell, I don't know. What does it look like to you?"

"It looks like he opened a bottle of beer and a tornado came out. Look at those things stuck in Donner's back."

"Yeah, I know," Hanley replied thickly.

"And the bits of wood and metal shot into the walls, and here, in the broken table top." Sturdevent looked grimly at his colleague. That isn't natural. A person can't do that, it takes too much force and pressure on a tiny point."

"Do you think it could have been some kind of explosion or—"

"No, not an explosion. Nothing looks burned. No smell. Some kind of freak whirlwind, maybe."

"Indoors?" Hanley sounded unconvinced. He still wanted to establish human agency.

"I know it sounds unlikely, but it's the only thing I can think of that makes any kind of sense."

"Look at the window frames," Hanley countered. "They're both three-quarters shut and they blew out in that position. No whirlwind or dust devil could have come in through those narrow openings and then done all this."

"Yeah, well. Back door? Who knows, damn it all. I'm going down to call for some outside help."

"Who?" Hanley asked, one eyebrow raised in mild surprise. "I don't know yet. Waterbury or Hartford, or the State Police. All this stuff has to be examined by a good lab crew and we just don't have the facilities to do it."

"That's the truth. You going to talk to the Feds?"

"They'll be notified, of course. Donner was a federal employee. But I don't think we have to ask them to investigate. Yet."

"Chief? What do you want me to do?"

"Stay here and search the rest of the apartment, Ned. I'll send Dave back up to watch this room. Don't let Doc Schmidt disturb things any more than he has to in examining the body."

"Right."

"I'll get some lab boys over here as soon as possible."

On his way to the station Sturdevent's mind was a jumble of confused thoughts. He would have to tell them about Bondarevsky's cow. Tomorrow or the next day. He wanted to see a complete lab report on the room, first, and a post-mortem from Doc Schmidt. Then they could sit down and try to make sense of it all. But as he rode along the darkening streets of Millville, he worried.

There was a sick, inescapable feeling in his gut that something was happening to his town. Something terrible. Something he might not be able to handle.

———

"I'm going inside and see if there's a ball game on TV, honey." Stu Calder said, rising from the lawn chair.

"Okay, lover."

"Want anything?"

"No, I'll be in soon." Marge Calder swirled the last inch of whiskey sour in a stem glass.

"The grass is damp, watch out for the night-crawlers between your toes," Stu said

"They don't bother me." She heard the screen door click shut behind her husband. It was a glorious night. The sky was brilliant with stars and the air was still warm but not at all uncomfortable. There was even a hint of a breeze up from the valley.

Marge Calder was twenty-five, three years younger than her husband who was already a very successful systems analyst. They had built this house on Riverside Hill the year before. It had cost a lot, but it was worth it—the view was one of the best in the area. They were here to stay, Marge knew that. Stu didn't mind the drive to New Haven every day. They wanted to live in a small town, in a special house, their very own house.

Sometimes Marge regretted it a little. Millville was pretty dull compared with New Haven, where she and Stu had met and married, and even New Haven was pretty dull compared with other cities she had been to. But you could always drive to New York for a little excitement, dinner and a show. The peace and quiet here was worth it. When her parents had split up, years ago, she decided that she would have and hold a family, her family, in her home. She always thought that neither of her parents ever really wanted her, they were so caught up in their own lives.

That would never happen in her family, the one she was going to have. But she didn't believe in rushing children. There was plenty of time for that. Now was the time when she and Stu could enjoy each other and their freedom. The house now; in a few years the children.

She inhaled deeply, enjoying the clear air. She still wore the skimpy bikini and white terry-cloth robe she had on when they returned from a swim at the lake earlier in the evening. The night is delicious, she thought, walking barefoot through the cool, moist grass towards the back end of their lawn. They had over an acre of land, though some of it sloped away sharply at the rear of the lot. Marge liked the tall grass and weeds that grew there. The rough edge was nice, more interesting that a perfectly manicured plot, which was what all the other yards in the area were. She liked the country feel, even if it was largely illusion.

She sat down in the tall grass now. Her long, tanned legs were slick with moisture and she rubbed them slowly, with pleasure. Marge enjoyed her body, sex was healthy, fun, just about the best thing she could think of. Stu liked to watch her caress herself and she enjoyed doing it. She lay back in the tall grass and gazed at the sky dreamily. Some night she and Stu would have to come out here and make love. He could be persuaded. Some night soon. At midnight, that would be nice. Marge swung her arms around in half-circles, splashing more water from the surrounding plants onto her face and body. She felt wonderful, cool and silvery, a night nymph.

When she sat up a few minutes later and looked out across the valley, she saw the bright blue light almost immediately.

Gosh, she thought, that's what Sylvia and I saw the other day. The light was in about the same place, on the opposite side of the valley. It seemed much brighter now, at night. Again, Marge found it impossible to tell whether it was on the ground or in the air—at this distance and against the receding backdrop of a hilly landscape the perspective was too difficult to make out. But it looks like it's in the air, hovering, she thought.

"Stu—" she started to call out, but stopped, knowing he wouldn't hear her. Even if he did he probably wouldn't come right away, not if he was watching a ball game. She rose to go get her husband and, in turning to the house, she spotted another blue light, far to the north of the town.

"Wow." She breathed the word. Although the second light was farther away it seemed almost as bright as the other one. It also seemed certainly to be in the air, just above the line of the land as she tried to picture it. They were beautiful, but they couldn't be man-made, she thought, and the notion of flying saucers crossed her mind again, just as it had the other day. Marge was a firm believer in flying saucers. Just looking at the stars on any night, a night like tonight, was enough to convince her that there was life elsewhere. And all those sightings, they couldn't *all* be disproved. The only problem was, flying saucers were supposed to fly, and those things just sat there. Hovering? Studying us? Endless possibilities raced through her mind. She scanned the view in all directions, hoping for more bright lights, but the southern exposure was obscured less than a mile away by the bend of the hill, and to the west, over the roof of her house, the Calders' own large horse-chestnut trees reached up to the stars.

Marge felt a shiver run through her, and she remained staring at the twin blue flares for a few more moments before trotting across the back lawn and into the house. It took five minutes and a commercial before she got Stu outside. The lights were still there.

"See," she said, pointing to the first light she had seen.

"Oh yeah," he said, "yeah, I see it." He didn't sound overly impressed.

"And there," she pointed to the other light in the north. "See? Just like the other one."

"Yeah, you're right, honey."

"What do you think they could be?"

"Neon signs, obviously," he replied as if that were the only possible explanation.

"Stuart, they aren't neon signs."

"Sure they are, Marge." He patted her backside playfully.

"Well I saw that one the other day, in broad daylight, and so did Sylvia Berkovitz."

"So?"

"Who turns on lights during the day?"

"Lots of people. Besides, they're probably new and maybe they were trying them out the other day."

"I don't think so. Up there," she pointed north, "there's nothing but woods and back roads anyhow. Who'd put a sign out there?"

"I don't know, maybe it can be seen from the highway. Come on inside, honey."

"Oh, Stuart, the highway's miles away."

"You can't tell from here, Marge, things look out of whack at night."

"Well, those just don't look like neon signs to me."

"Okay, what do you think they are?"

Marge frowned to herself. She knew Stu would just chuckle if she started talking about flying saucers, especially if they didn't fly.

"Come on inside. There's a good game on and I'm missing it." He started to walk back to the house.

Marge continued looking at the lights for a few seconds, and then followed her husband. Maybe they were signs, but she didn't think so. She would just have to find out.

"Misadventure." Chief Sturdevent said the word flatly, without enthusiasm. He pushed a paper-clip about his desk with one finger.

"Misadventure?" Martin Lasker raised his eyebrows in surprise. "That sounds like something from a British detective story."

"Maybe," Sturdevent said neutrally.

"But misadventure means, as I understand the term, an accident. It doesn't apply to what happened to Donner."

"It's the only thing we can call it, at this time." Sturdevent carefully stressed the last three words. "We simply have nothing else to go on."

"But a man was brutally, savagely killed."

"That's right."

"You can't just call that misadventure, Chief."

"What else can we call it? It sure wasn't suicide. It wasn't natural causes."

"Why not call it murder, pure and simple?"

"Because." Sturdevent sighed wearily. "It doesn't necessarily add up as murder. Donner had no enemies we can find a trace of, there was no motive and the whole way he died is all wrong for murder. There would have had to be a gang of them in that room to do all that damage. Well, there just isn't a bunch of escaped psychotics on the loose in the state; in fact there haven't been any escapes lately."

"They don't have to be escaped. You haven't got all the nuts locked up around the country by any means."

"I know that, but you're missing my point. Let me put it this way, Martin. Even a band of murderers probably couldn't have done the things that happened in that apartment—wood slivers drilled into the baseboard and so on; the guy's scalp ripped up."

Lasker shifted in his seat across the desk from Chief Sturdevent. "Do you think it ties in with what happened to Bondarevsky's cow?"

"Off the record, yes, I think it does." Sturdevent pushed the paper-clip to one side and folded his large hands on his belly, unconsciously covering his growing roll of fat. "In fact, I'm almost certain the two incidents are related, but at the moment that doesn't help us at all. You saw Bondarevsky's cow and you've seen these photos of Donner." The Chief nudged a small pile of repulsive black-and-white police photographs on his desk. "What would you make of it all?" Sturdevent paused briefly before continuing. "So you don't like Doc Schmidt's verdict. If you or anybody else has any ideas or suggestions or even a genuine clue, I'd be happy to hear about it." He even managed a thin smile.

Lasker glanced at the photos again and then turned away quickly. They were not a pleasant sight and he was glad he had not actually been in the Hoadley Street apartment. "Yeah, well. When we were out at Bondarevsky's I thought what had happened to his cow was just some odd thing. I couldn't accept his remarks about some fiendish butcher doing it."

"But," Sturdevent prompted.

"But now, with Donner, there's a repetition, a pattern. It still seems outrageous and impossible but it no longer seems like an accident."

"I agree completely," Sturdevent said. "But that still doesn't give me anything to go on. It could still be some kind of freak happening."

"Lightning striking twice?"

Sturdevent merely shrugged.

Lasker found himself growing annoyed with the Chiefs stolid, complacent attitude. It stumped him but there was little he could do about it. Tough. Maybe it'll go away.

"Now I think it has to be the work of some person or persons unknown," Lasker asserted. "I can see there are problems, some of the things you mention in the apartment, but I can't see Donner just dying in that way. It's crazy, impossible."

"You ought to be on the police force, son—no, I'm sorry if that sounded patronizing. It's good that you have questions and won't accept the first answer that comes along. I have questions, we all have questions. Questions are healthy, a teacher of mine once said. But the trouble is, it's nice to have the occasional answer, the occasional *right* answer. It's my job to find the right answers, and in this situation we have a whole lot of questions and not one single goddamn halfway-to-solid answer for anything. Nothing fits.

"Look at Bondarevsky's cow. Who would go out there and do that to some cow? Not even a crazy would do it that way. Hell, we've even thought about witchcraft—some folks still mess around with it—but there'd be signs, and there weren't any. They'd do it some place special. Out at Dayton's Den, maybe. But the way it actually did happen, it doesn't fit anything at all.

"Look at Donner. A nobody, a meek, mild slob who kept to himself, didn't drink, held a steady job in the post office, living in a tiny dump over a pizza parlor, for Christ's sake. Why him? Far as we can tell, all he ever did outside work was play chess and jerk off. All those Russian things, they were all just chess writings, nothing more, so bang goes the dumb theory that he was involved in some kind of espionage work—yeah, you laugh. I told you we've considered everything under the sun." Sturdevent sighed heavily, perhaps surprised by the length of his own speech.

"So now..." Lasker raised his eyebrows.

"So now we've had a heap of destruction and a violent death, and we can't buy a clue. That's so now."

"Have you had a lab report?"

"We had two quote guest unquote detectives in from Waterbury, yeah, and a lab crew. You know we just don't have the facilities and staff here in Millville to do that kind of work."

"I know. What did they find."

"Nothing at all. No prints, except those of Donner and a couple of his pals. Nothing unusual, nothing that wasn't already in the room. No sign of an explosion. They took away a few bags full of wreckage from the apartment for more detailed examination and testing."

"Maybe something will come from that."

"Maybe, but I doubt it. This case has a lousy feel to it. Nothing is going our way."

"And you're satisfied that everything that can be done is being done?"

The Chief stiffened. "What the hell do you think?"

———

Pomar had not exaggerated: the children were unshakeable. But Father Lombardy, in his half-hour talk with them, had detected soft spots. He was mildly surprised to find that Maria was by far the more talkative of the two on the subject. She was quite sure she had seen Mary, the Mother of God. She heard voices, but she didn't know what they said. Once, the first time, they had felt the touch of Mary; on subsequent occasions they stayed back several yards. She had appeared to them a few times now, but not every day. What especially interested Father Lombardy about Maria's testimony was that she could not say what Mary looked like, nor even whether She appeared simply as a face or with a complete body. Maria would only say that She was there, in the center of a wondrous blue cloud.

Joey, on the other hand, was even less precise, although he was equally insistent that the experiences they described were genuine. He agreed that it had been Mary who appeared to them, but he said this with slightly less fervor than his sister. The priest tried to probe more deeply, but the boy refused to be drawn. He seemed to be easily irritated and more than once he asked why, if Father Lombardy was a Catholic priest, he was so suspicious of the visitations. Didn't he believe? The priest explained patiently that Christ or Mary appeared to man on Earth only very rarely, and then only for some very important reason. The children greeted this comment with silence.

Joey was also vague on the subject of the voices. Whereas his sister described them as beautiful, musical and heavenly, Joey would only say that yes, he had heard something that could be a voice or voices, but he didn't know what it meant. Didn't he think that if Mary was speaking to them She would speak in a way they could understand? Joey again said nothing but Maria exclaimed 'Yes' enthusiastically, as if the Virgin's failure to do so annoyed her, too.

Joey admitted he too had felt the touch of Mary on him that first day. They had fallen to the ground and he had begun praying. He didn't know how many prayers he had said but at some point he noticed the silence and the calm around them. They looked up and were alone again.

As far as Father Lombardy was concerned, the meeting was inconclusive and just a little unnerving. He hadn't expected the children to be as unyielding as they were. Also, he had expected them to trot out fairly familiar descriptions, incidents, features like a halo — the kind of things they might easily pick up from potted biographies of the saints or booklets about Lourdes and Fatima. But they hadn't done so. The blurred and fuzzy edges to their collective account added credence to their story rather than detracted from it.

And the way they innocently threw their faith back at him, the priest, also lodged in his mind at an awkward angle. Didn't he believe? In his religion, yes, of course. And in his priesthood, yes. But miracles? Heavenly visitations? Had he ever even thought about it much? Church history was rich with such astounding events so why should it seem such a strange notion now?

Father Lombardy left the Pomar house that evening feeling as if he had stepped off a neat suburban patio into a swampy field, and muddy water was leaking into his shiny cordovan shoes.

Later that night he briefly discussed the matter with Father Connors, the eldest of the four priests at St Jude's, and the pastor of the parish. Father Lombardy gave only the barest details and asked if he was handling the situation in the best way. The old priest listened with a flicker of a sly smile hovering at the corners of his eyes. But some of Father Lombardy's unease was communicated in spite of the fact that he tried to mask it behind a sober, straight-forward attitude, and Father Connors poured two glasses of port before speaking.

"The Church finds this kind of thing terribly embarrassing," he said.

After that it was all downhill. He rambled on for several minutes in his weak, throaty voice. He was no help to Father Lombardy, saying virtually the same things and in almost the same order as the younger priest had first said to Art Pomar. Father Lombardy listened politely, nodding his head frequently, realizing that he was going to hear nothing new. The pastor was sincere and well-intentioned, but that was about it.

His last comment had been "Lay it to rest quickly, William, or they'll be seriously disturbed." Those words echoed in his mind now as Father Lombardy walked across the football field at the back of Emerson School with Joey Pomar. He felt like a religious CIA operative on assignment to a trouble-spot.

"Where's your sister today, Joey?"

"Mom kept her home today," the youth replied sullenly. He didn't look very happy to be seen by his classmates walking off into the woods with a priest, and Father Lombardy thought it must look strange. He certainly felt strange.

"This looks like a good place to play," the priest said as they followed the path. The boy said nothing. "Are there many animals in these woods, Joey?"

"Woodchucks, squirrels, grass snakes… less and less."

"Less and less? Why?"

"They're starting to clear the land to build houses or something. Not many animals left."

When they came to the rocky outcrop Joey moved faster and the priest kept pace. Joey came to the cliff edge and stood fearlessly looking down.

"Nope, not there," the boy said clearly.

"That's a fair drop. Down there, is that where you and Maria saw it?"

"Her," Joey corrected. "Yep, right there. The blue cloud reached almost up to the top here."

"Nothing there now, is there?" Father Lombardy tried to ask the question in a totally neutral tone, so as not to annoy the child.

"Nope," Joey replied simply.

"Can we go down and take a closer look?"

"Sure. This way."

Joey led the priest to the far edge and then down the narrow path that wound around the stone face. They reached the clearing in a few moments. Father Lombardy strode into the center of the clearing and turned around.

"Right here, Joey?"

"Yes, Father." The boy had held back at the edge of the clearing at first, but now walked slowly up to the priest.

"Must be a twenty, twenty-five foot drop," Father Lombardy said gazing up the cliff wall. "Where were you and Maria," he said, turning to the boy, "when you—?"

The wind caught them both and flung them through the air into the brush at the perimeter of the clearing; The speed and violence of the action stunned the priest, but he recovered quickly, scrambling on all fours.

"See!" Joey cried from a few feet away.

Father Lombardy grabbed the boy, pressing him to the ground beneath him. "Is that it?" he whispered hoarsely, knowing that it was.

Blue, fiery light blossomed in front of the cliff.

In it, filling it, were faces.

PART TWO
THE CLOUD OF UNKNOWING

"The ghost of electricity
Howls in the bones of her face."
– Bob Dylan

CHAPTER FIVE

Martin Lasker drove past the broad green fairways of the Millville golf course and turned into a quiet, attractive street canopied with tall elms and maples. The houses on Field Street were large and expensive, a strange mixture of restored colonial homes and modem split-level palaces, with a second and sometimes a third car in almost every driveway, expansive lawns and more swimming pools on this golden mile than in the rest of the entire town. Natural timber fences added a rustic touch.

Lasker thought it odd that Doc Schmidt should live in this neighborhood. By all accounts, the physician's practice was not the liveliest in Millville, nor the wealthiest. Obviously he wouldn't continue acting as the town coroner and medical examiner, which was a poorly paid job, if he didn't need the money. How did he manage to buy a house out here in the first place? Perhaps, years ago, Schmidt had inherited some money.

The doctor's house-and-office was one of the most handsome on the street, a rambling white colonial edifice that bore the date 1792. But, as Lasker walked up the drive, he noticed that the paint was beginning to peel in one or two spots and the front lawn needed mowing. The only other car in sight was Schmidt's own Chrysler, which Lasker guessed to be about twelve years old.

Lasker rang the bell and after some minutes was greeted by a woman about his own age. She looked vaguely surprised to see him. She wore a candy-stripe nurse's uniform that seemed somehow inappropriate and her white cap was perched on an enormous sweep of teased, dirty-blonde hair. To Lasker she looked like a seven-foot amazon. After that flicker of hesitation, she unleashed a broad, toothy smile.

"Come on in." She stood back and waved her arm.

"Thank you."

The young woman led Lasker into a small reception room that contained three chairs and a settee in what is loosely described as the Scandinavian style, and her desk, behind which she moved. Lasker remained standing.

When she had composed herself, the receptionist said, "Can I help you?"

"I've come to see Doctor Schmidt," the reporter said, thinking it should be fairly obvious.

"Do you have an appointment?"

"I phoned him, yes, he knows I'm coming."

"Your name, sir?"

"Martin Lasker, but," as she scanned a lean appointments book, "I'm not a patient"

"Oh," she said looking up, her face now troubled. "Are you a salesman?"

"No, I work for the *Millville News*. I'm here to see the doctor on personal business."

"Oh, I see." The toothy smile returned. "Do sit down, won't you?" She waved her arm again, theatrically.

Lasker sat on the edge of one of the chairs and noticed for the first time the triangular nameplate on the receptionist's desk. It read: Miss K. Peters. He looked up at Miss K. Peters and found she was still smiling blankly at him.

"Is the doctor in?" he asked after a pause.

"Oh, yes," she said quickly, shaking her head as if coming out of a trance. "He's in the toilet, but he should be out soon."

Good God, Lasker thought, where did Schmidt find this creature? If she acted like this all the time it was no wonder the appointments book had so few entries. He smiled thinly back at her.

"You're—Miss Peters?" He nodded towards the nameplate.

"Yes, that's me. Are you writing a story about Doctor Schmidt?" Her eyebrows arched in a serious attempt to strike a reflective pose.

"No, I just want to get some medical information from him. Background, you know."

"Oh yeah, I see."

"Are you a nurse?" he asked fearfully after a few more moments of silence.

"No, I'm just the doctor's receptionist. He doesn't have a nurse. Sometimes I help him, sterilizing instruments or stuff like that, but mostly I'm out here."

"I see."

Again, a few moments of silence. Miss Peters stared at Lasker as if he were some unusual specimen in a display case.

"Did you go to Millie?" she asked, referring to the local high school.

"Yes, I did."

"So did I, but I don't remember seeing you there."

"I was probably before your time."

Miss Peters looked as if she were about to disagree, but then thought better of it. "When did you—?" She was interrupted by the sound of a door slamming somewhere in the house. "Oh, he's out of the john now. I'll tell him you're here." She rose from her seat and strode out of the room. Within a few seconds she had returned, her head peering in through the doorway from the hall. "The doctor will see you now," she said with a smile, in what was apparently intended to be her best professional tone of voice. She led Lasker down the hall, past a storeroom crammed with cardboard cartons, past a small room with a large flat patient's bed in the center, to an office. Miss Peters stood by the door and gestured. "Please go right in."

"Thank you," Lasker said as he passed her. The door clicked shut behind him.

"So. Mr. Lasker. How do you do?" Doctor E. E. Schmidt, a tall, gaunt, cadaverous individual of middle years, stepped forward and shook hands with the reporter. With his pallid complexion and his too-large laboratory coat, the physician looked like an enormous white penguin.

"Fine, doctor, thank you."

"Sit down, sit down." He motioned Lasker to a plain wooden chair beside his desk, which was so small that when Schmidt sat down behind it he made Lasker think of someone who had been trapped in grammar school all his life. "Sorry about it being so dark in here. I have to get the damn fluorescent light fixed. They're always on the fritz."

"Not at all." Lasker looked briefly around. It was a splendid room furnished in appalling style. Even the yellowed diploma on the wall was slightly out of kilter.

"What can I do for you?"

"Well, sir, I work for the *Millville News*, as I think I told you on the phone."

"Yes, yes, I remember. Proceed." Schmidt sat forward over the desk, with a serious, business-like look on his face.

"I wanted to ask you a few questions about the death of James Donner."

"Ah, yes. Tragic matter."

"Yes, it was." Lasker cleared his throat. "However there—"

"But I already gave my report, Mr. Lasker. Surely you can check with the town authorities."

"Yes, sir, I've seen your report, but it still leaves a lot of questions in my mind."

"I see, I see." The doctor's eyes widened with fascination. "You think there was something more to it?"

"Well, don't you?"

"Of course," Schmidt replied with an off-hand shrug, closing his eyes briefly.

"Well, what do you mean by misadventure? What is your professional understanding of the term?" The physician raised his eyebrows in annoyance, and Lasker quickly added: "I want to make sure I understand the exact meaning of the word in the medical and legal senses."

Somewhat mollified, Schmidt leaned back and stared into space, explaining, "Misadventure is an unlucky accident, unlucky, indeed often fatal. In fact, in the legal sense, strictly speaking, it is always fatal, otherwise it's assault and battery and who cares anyhow? Best example, the textbook example, is when a household cat jumps into the baby's crib because it is attracted by the smell of milk. Cat falls asleep on baby's face, smothering baby. Death by misadventure. Hardly ever happens, but there you are. Good example."

"But it has to be an accident?"

"Accident, chance, that sort of thing. The absence of design, you see. If you were bitten by a bushmaster, you—"

"A what?"

"A bushmaster, Mr. Lasker. It's a snake, a wonderful snake from South America. Also known as *Lachesis muta*. It can reach twelve feet in length, and its bite is especially deadly, in a very nasty way. So."

Doctor Schmidt lapsed into silence and that faraway, dreamy look returned to his eyes. The tiniest hint of a smile suggested itself at the corners of his lips. Lasker waited patiently for a few moments before interrupting.

"Doctor Schmidt?"

"Yes, yes," he murmured, coming around slowly. "I was just thinking of that bushmaster. Such a snake. You know, the venom of the bushmaster renders the victim's neck muscles inoperative so he can't control his head. It just rolls around on the neck any which way—like so." The physician proceeded to roll his head around, and let his tongue hang out for good measure. "And then, of course, they die. But that neck effect is remarkable. I wonder why a snake would evolve a venom with such a special, localised effect?"

"We were talking about misadventure, sir," Martin Lasker said as politely as he could manage.

"Yes, well," Doctor Schmidt took up instantly, switching back into his lecturing manner. "If you were camping out—in the tropics, of course—and a bushmaster came into your tent and bit you and you died, that we could call death by misadventure. But if someone put the snake in your tent, well, that would naturally be murder. You see? Accident. Design. A murder like that would be very hard to prove, but you'd have the problem of getting the damn snake to the tent without having it bit you first. Not so simple, eh?"

"What bothers me about the Donner case, sir, is—"

"Yes, Donner, yes."

"Yes, uh, what bothers me is that what happened in that room seems hard to describe as an accident."

"Ah, yes, well…" Schmidt let the words trail away. He looked philosophical.

"I mean, I didn't see the body, but I did see the room, and all that destruction—it just wasn't an accident."

"I can see how you might think that, Mr. Lasker, but you would like it even less if I had called it death by natural causes."

"You couldn't have done that."

"Well... I don't suppose I could have, but all the available evidence indicates it was not caused by human agency—not that I would entirely rule out that possibility, you understand. I could have rendered an open verdict, I suppose, but I don't like doing that, and misadventure is not, as I have tried to show you, inappropriate or inaccurate. It can remain an open case in the police files, but not in mine."

"It's just not complete."

"What's not complete? What are natural causes, for that matter? What is cancer? A disease, or simply a new form of self-destruction, an evolutionary check?"

Lasker had a grim vision of Schmidt continuing on, growing more and more speculative in his monologue, so he hastily spoke up.

"About the body, sir, I read in your catalogue of things that happened—the broken bones and so on."

"So much."

"Yes, exactly, but I couldn't figure out from your report which specific occurrence in the body brought about death."

"Neither could I," the physician answered simply. "There was so much—the heart, the brain, the spine—you can take your pick. I don't know the actual chronology of the disaster."

"If you had to guess? Off the record, of course."

"Off the record I would still find it hard to guess. Maybe the spine went first, maybe the skull. Who knows?"

Lasker sighed. So far he had made very few notes in his pad. "Do you know of anything, again off the record, all this is just for me to think about, sir, you won't be quoted, unless of course you want to be—do you know of anything that could do or cause that kind of damage in a person?"

"It could be done by other people, but it is so utterly unlikely that the possibility doesn't merit serious consideration. It would take almost superhuman strength and control. Mr. Lasker, a chess pawn has a round ball for a cap. To drive it through the skin, through the muscle and fat, into the spine at an oblique angle, without making an incision first or using a hammer, which would leave a much larger bruise than actually was found—well, the more I think about it the less I believe that any person is physically able to do that."

"All right, after seeing the room I find it hard to imagine anyone doing that. But where does that leave us?"

"If I knew, Mr. Lasker, it would be in my report. As for idle guesses—a whirlwind perhaps? Tornados have driven pieces of straw through planks of pinewood. It's possible, and if so, that's misadventure."

"A whirlwind indoors? I'm not a meteorologist, but—"

"Listen, anything's possible. Last year in England a housewife reported that she was cooking in the kitchen when a fireball floated in through the open window and brushed up against her, scorching her dress."

"Well, that—' Lasker made a dismissive gesture with his hand.

"Yes, yes, it's quite possible, believe me. Not a publicity stunt by a crank. There have been a number of similar incidents here and in Europe. They think it has to do with electric stoves or microwave ovens and ionized air. They are investigating now." Schmidt emphasized the last word by tapping a finger on his desk as if he expected a final report any minute. "But the fireball effect is apparently quite possible, and if that can happen, indoors as well as out, then who knows what might have happened to poor Mr. Donner?"

"Do you recall when last year this happened?" Lasker asked, intending to check the paper's files for a news item on it.

"Summer, maybe autumn? If she had the window open, in England, it must have been summer. Maybe late summer."

"Thanks. So you think the Donner case was just a freakish accident?"

"Yes. Not an accident in the every-day sense of the word, but a very unusual accident. Yes."

"Was there anything you noticed in your examination of the body, anything that still troubles you? Something you might have left out of your report because it seemed too vague or tenuous?"

"Everybody wants a clue," Schmidt said with a smile, "a clue to set them on the trail. I'm sorry I don't have any." The doctor tore a blank sheet from the prescription pad on his desk, rolled it into a ball and tossed it into the wicker wastebasket several feet away. "If you want something to think about, Mr. Lasker, think about this. Maybe our fine technological world has gotten so far out of hand that things can begin to happen that we don't even recognize or understand. Impossible things, like this."

Lasker decided to file that line of speculation for thought at some other time. "If I told you that the same sort of thing happened only a few days before the Donner incident, only it happened to an animal— would you still think it was a freak accident?"

Lasker was annoyed with himself for not realizing that Sturdevent would naturally discuss the Bondarevsky matter with Schmidt. A duff reporter's question. "So we have two incidents in a short space of time in the same area."

"That's right."

"That makes it less freakish, doesn't it?"

"Not really, Mr. Lasker. The fact that it happened to the cow reinforces my opinion rather than weakens it. Perhaps some freak topological effect, something in the air."

Martin Lasker wrote on his pad: *Something in the air.* Schmidt and Sturdevent had worked out this line together, and it reminded him of politicians who, during the war in Vietnam, spoke of the light at the end of the tunnel As if it were real. As if it were an answer. The politicians had been selling an illusion. The notion that the cow and James Donner had been killed by a freak of nature seemed to Lasker to be the same kind of wishful thinking. But he had no explanations either.

After a few more inconsequential questions and equally inconsequential answers, Lasker rose to leave. "Thanks very much for your time, Doctor."

"Not at all. I'm sorry if I wasn't able to help you much."

"It's a very puzzling, disturbing problem."

"Yes, it is. I hope you solve it for us." Doctor Schmidt shook Lasker's hand lingeringly. "By the way, Mr. Lasker, just while you're here."

"Yes?"

"Have you had a physical check-up lately? You should have one every six months, you know."

Lasker realized suddenly that Doctor Schmidt was taking his pulse. "Yes, as a matter of fact, I have. And a chest X-ray."

Schmidt released Lasker's wrist without the slightest trace of self-consciousness, and gave the reporter a hearty slap on the back.

"Good, good."

Miss Peters was reading *Myra Breckinridge* as Lasker passed through the reception room.

"Good-bye."

"Come again," she smiled sweetly.

———

The ceiling was patterned with circles. Perhaps the color had originally been sunshine yellow or a brisk mustard or even a pure, glossy white, but time had steadily dulled it to a lifeless gold. This was a good old building, or had been. Rooms meant to control, define and dominate space. Layout designed to marshal and channel activity into regular form and practice.

Solidity.

To support.

To enhance.

To house.

To shelter.

Now it just seemed angular and boxlike. A tired shell. The hush no longer suggested reverence or wisdom; it was the joyless silence of sterility.

Father Lombardy rolled over and sat up on the edge of his bed. He crushed out a cigarette. After five months he was smoking again.

What would Thomas Merton say about today's event? Or Paul Tillich, or Martin Buber, or, better still, the old demythologizer Rudolf Bultmann? The young priest scanned the books on his shelf and an image grew in his mind: dozens of learned elderly men, philosophers, theologians, scientists, all sitting calmly in deck-chairs around the clearing, watching the blue fire and faces of heaven or hell that had confronted Father Lombardy. Would they nod, whisper to each other, or simply jump up and run through the swampy undergrowth, as he had this afternoon?

Ridiculous. He shook himself out of the day-dream, rose, walked over to the small writing desk, turned over a letter from his mother so that the blank backside of the page faced up, returned to his bed, sat down, lit up another Kent and leaned back against the headboard.

For the fiftieth time, he began to go over in his mind everything that had happened in that brief visit. It had all taken place so quickly. He should have stayed where he had fallen. Stayed and watched. Kept the faith, he thought, and that popular phrase now had an especially bitter taste. But he hadn't stayed. When he had seen Joey's eyes, wide, glassy, reacting with awe and enthusiasm, he had bolted, dragging the child with him. As he ran, fear began to rattle through his system and it was a physical as well as a mental thing, like a small but wild .22 bullet puncturing organs and bouncing off bones to do further damage. It hadn't let up.

Maybe there wasn't a logical explanation, maybe he was simply fortifying the trap he felt caught in, by seeking to reduce the experience to cold, dispassionate analysis. Analysis he was incapable of, anyhow. What was his basic, instinctive response? To run, to hide. But emotionally, psychologically, what visceral reaction? Fear. Yes, but what is behind the fear? What informs the fear? The unknown. The blue light. The faces. Forget the blue light, forget the shadowy faces, they're only the outward manifestation. What was communicated to you, what flashed like a laser beam to your psyche in that first awful moment of confrontation? Something you have been trying already to bury beneath layers of objective explanation, each more irrelevant and obstructing than the last

"Evil," he said, and the sound of his own clear voice startled him.

But that was what he had sensed immediately. Evil. Not clammy, fiendish, bloodcurdling evil, not the common, even fashionable notion of Satanic evil, the Devil and all his works. No, this was something bleak, desolate, impersonal, something removed from the lore of demonology. Is it possible for evil to exist in the abstract, he wondered?

Father Lombardy got up from his bed again, and walked across the room to his closet door. He looked at the poster reproduction of

Vermeer's *The Cook* which was mounted there. With his thumb he pressed hard on the tack in the lower left hand corner until it was flush with the door.

But maybe his gut feeling was wrong. After all, there had been nothing abstract about what he actually experienced out there today. He had been physically thrown through the air. For several feet. That action had been directed against himself and the boy. To make matters worse, that was precisely the sort of thing that suggested a poltergeist. Maybe the traditional tales had some substance. Certainly the Church did not openly say that ghosts and the like did not exist, although it frowned on the subject. The fact that the thing had been a blue light or a blue fire didn't necessarily matter; the common idea of a ghost as a kind of semi-transparent white nimbus of a wraith was not something you could look up in an encyclopedia and find verified as universal law. And there were the faces.

But poltergeists were said to be harmless, prankish spirits, and that didn't sit well with the priest. That sense of evil was too great to be denied. And being thrown through the air was a personal act, particularly if it happened that the thing was a force… a conscious and knowing presence… something… some thing.

It was hopeless. Father Lombardy felt as unsure of himself as he had this afternoon driving back to the rectory, his mind a turmoil.

He had to do something. He knew that. The Pomar kids were right about there being something at that place, and he would have to do something about it. Art Pomar had been on the phone twice already this evening, maybe more—Father Lombardy had told Mrs. Baukus he didn't feel well and didn't want to take any calls tonight. That had not gone down well with the old lady, who believed that a priest should always be on tap. Tomorrow. Tomorrow, he knew, he would have to do something.

At nine o'clock, Father Slomcenski knocked once, stuck his long hangdog face in the doorway and asked if Father Lombardy wanted to go down to the basement and play a few games of table tennis. Father Lombardy declined, saying he wanted to write some letters and go to bed early. He went on brooding.

Just after four in the morning he opened his eyes and realized he had fallen asleep with his clothes on. He felt hot and sticky with sweat.

As he groggily undressed he told himself that the Pomar children had to be kept away from that place. And he had to do something.

He would have to return there.

"I'm telling you, the way that chick sits there, day after day..." Dave Lutz stood in the kitchen of his apartment, a full bottle of vodka in one hand and a full bottle of KC tonic water in the other. On the Formica counter behind him was a cardboard box containing several other bottles of liquor and mixers. "Knees back and forth," he continued with a sly smile on his face. "Ever so gently, ever so innocently, one crotch shot after another." He swung his hands together and then apart in a slow but steady rhythm. "Jee-zuzz!"

Martin Lasker grinned broadly. He leaned back against the wall by the kitchen table. "Does she have any brains?"

"Enough to know what she's doing to me."

"If it's so bad, why don't you move her to a seat in the back of the room?" Lasker's grin wouldn't go away. He enjoyed listening to Lutz's weekly list of complaints about teaching. The two had been neighborhood friends through grammar school and high school in Millville, and now that they were both back working in their home town they got together a couple of times a week for a meal, or to listen to music and drink.

"Move her to the back of the room?" Lutz looked at Lasker incredulously. "Are you kidding—and miss all that?" He moved his hands back and forth again. "It's the only thing that gets me through to eleven o'clock and coffee."

"Uh-hunh. Are you going to stand there with those bottles all night, dreaming of Angie Allen's thighs, or are you going to make me a drink?"

"Right. I'm going to make drinks," Lutz replied, turning to the counter. "Don't worry, I'm in complete control." He took two large glasses from the cabinet in front of him and began pouring generous measures of vodka in each.

"When do you finish for the summer?" Lasker asked.

"Eleven working days, a mere eternity."

"That's not bad."

"Easy for you to say. I'm the one who has to face those dunderheads. Honestly, most of them are so dim they make Cheeta the chimp look like Einstein." Lutz shut the freezer door and handed Lasker a drink. "Try that."

Lasker sipped from the tumbler. "Strong. It's almost pure vodka."

"Drink up. Life is hard."

They moved from the kitchen to the living room, which was cluttered with newspapers, magazines, half-open paperback books, a carton of ginseng capsules, dirty laundry, drinking glasses, record albums, dead potted plants, school papers and other items. Still lives like a college student, Lasker thought—as he did every time he visited his friend.

"Are you going to look for a summer job?"

"I don't know," Lutz answered. "I think what I'd really like to do is commit amnesia for the next two and a half months."

"Commit amnesia?"

"Sure. Wash out my head, but good. Then I'll be ready to start teaching the next crop in September and go through it all again. Those kids are too much. They aren't learning from me; I'm unlearning from them."

"Ah, bull," Lasker said amiably.

"I'm not kidding," Lutz said quickly. "The other day I stopped into Murph's to get a full tank of gas and when the guy came to my car I couldn't get a complete sentence out. Honestly. I couldn't form it in my head, it was like a total block, paralysis of the thought process behind the act of speaking." Lutz's eyes were wide with astonishment, as if he found his own story amazing to hear. "Normally I'm fluent enough, even glib, they tell me in the teachers' lounge, the bastards, but all I could say to this guy was "Gas... gas": Naturally the guy thought I was weird, he didn't know I work at the high school, right? So he says, "Yeah, what about it?" Finally I managed to say "Filleruplease," like that, one word. I need a long vacation. I don't think I'll look for a summer job," Lutz finished, suddenly arriving at an answer to Lasker's question.

"You need a woman."

"And how, but I won't find one in this town. Nothing here but old men, wild dogs and Barbie dolls, not to mention the real drawbacks. How about you? What's Millville's answer to Woodward and Bernstein doing these days?"

"The usual nonsense," Lasker said. "You'll be happy to hear that the Little League opened its season the other day."

"Never mind that. Have you found out who the mayor's fucking these days?"

"The taxpayers, as usual. They're going to put parking meters on Walnut Street, Hill Street and Echo Lake Road."

"Shit."

"My interview with the police chief about the problem with teenagers at the plaza was a bust"

"Really? I didn't see it."

"Because it didn't appear. It was so boring even the typesetter fell asleep halfway through it. Phippsy was kind-hearted about it when he told me he had reduced it from eleven hundred words to a one sentence paragraph saying the police promised action to prevent rowdies from causing trouble at the plaza."

"What the hell. Have another drink."

While Dave Lutz poured another round of drinks in the kitchen, Martin Lasker thumbed through a stack of records on the floor. Dave must spend all his extra money on albums and drink, he thought Not necessarily in that order. Lasker extracted a 1939 recording of Count Basie and Lester Young, and glanced down through the liner notes.

"What about that guy who died in a pizza parlor?" Lutz said, returning with the drinks.

"Above a pizza parlor," Lasker corrected. "Now that *is* interesting, but nobody can get a handle on it, so we've just been running the police statements—which say nothing in the usual way." He sipped the drink and found it as strong as the first one.

"Sounded pretty—ghoulish. From what I heard on the radio."

"It was. The poor bastard was torn to pieces, and the same thing happened to a cow only a few days before."

"A cow? You're kidding."

"No, honest"

"I didn't hear about that."

"The police and the medical examiner think it was some kind of violent wind, like a mini-tornado or something."

"Wind?" Dave Lutz sat forward in his chair. His brow wrinkled.

"Yeah, it sounded pretty feeble to me. If the cow had been out in a field, or Donner had been walking down the street—then, maybe. But both were indoors, so it's a hard theory to believe."

"I don't find it hard to believe. It happened to me."

"What?"

"The wind. Indoors."

"Are you kidding?" But Lasker sensed already that his friend meant it. Lutz faced him squarely, soberly.

"No. I'm telling you, I felt a strange wind, in the classroom one day, week before last." Lutz went on to relate the incident in the school. "It sounds trivial and insignificant, I know, but after what you said it makes me feel kind of nervous."

"Well," Lasker said, exhaling slowly, trying to digest what he had just heard. "That makes three times, if it's the same thing. Maybe four, if the car is related."

"What car?"

"Somebody's car was demolished the night before Donner died. Totally wrecked. It was parked in front of his house. I didn't see it, so I don't know. Everybody seems to think it was vandals, but the only witness, who apparently put down a lot of beer and isn't too reliable, claims nobody did it, that it just happened."

"A cow, a car, a dead man and some flapping papers on a schoolroom bulletin, board—it doesn't add up."

"No, it doesn't, but something's happening and it isn't very nice." Lasker's mind roamed over the unresolved items. After talking to Doctor Schmidt the reporter had put the matter aside, but hearing Lutz list the incidents again, one after another, adding his own experience with the putative wind, brought the whole thing crashing back into the forefront of his consciousness. And he didn't like that, because it seemed there was absolutely nothing he could do about it.

"So you've got a riddle, Marty. Things aren't so dull after all. But that wild wind idea sounds right to me. I don't know anything about weather, except not to stand out in the rain, but I suppose the wind can do strange things."

"You sound just like Sturdevent."

"Who's he?"

"The chief of police."

"Well, if the wind can blow up, I guess it can die down or blow away."

"Yeah, sure…"

"Why don't you call up the state weather bureau—where is it, Windsor Locks?—and ask somebody about how winds behave? Certainly more interesting than covering the next pitch-and-putt tournament."

"Maybe. But that's not all. Some woman has been calling up reporting flying saucers and I have to go talk to her."

"Terrific. If you want to see some green-eyed monsters, come on over to the high school. I have them by the roomful."

"No thanks."

"Well, I don't see why you're complaining, Marty, with all these strange doings in a small town. I ought to get in this newspaper business too—and I would, except I'm illiterate. Do you want some spaghetti?" Lutz rose and moved towards the kitchen.

"Not unless you have real tomato sauce. I'm tired of having to eat ketchup every time you make spaghetti."

"All right, already," Lutz shouted back over his shoulder. Lasker sat thinking. The ice melted in his vodka.

CHAPTER SIX

Church Street was one of several quiet thoroughfares on the periphery of Millville town center. It was largely residential but it contained a fair number of small shops and businesses that had spilled over from the main streets. The houses were old two-and three-story structures that dated from the Twenties and Thirties. Many of the ground floors had long since been converted into stores, but in recent years the trend had begun to reverse itself as townspeople made more and more use of the large shopping plazas that had sprung up around Millville and nearby towns. At any given time six or eight For Let or For Sale signs could be counted in the space of a couple of blocks.

Children played in the street, as front yards were virtually non-existent and the nearest playground was on the other side of the river, across Millville's famous Bailey Bridge. Famous because when it was built in the late Thirties it cost the citizens nearly as much as the Brooklyn Bridge. It was a simple steel girder construction, not much more sophisticated than something the United States Army might sling across a small river in wartime. There had been a scandal at the time but no one ever found out just whose pockets all that money had filled.

At six-thirty in the evening Church Street was pretty quiet. The business people had all gone home and most of the residents were inside finishing their meals. Dogs lazed on stoops. Even in summer, darkness gathered early here, as the street was at the base of the valley, adjacent to the river.

On this Monday evening, just after six-thirty, all the windows on one short block of Church Street blew out in rapid succession. Nine buildings were hit, including Ralph's Barber Shop and Shepard's Photographic Studio, which had large picture windows. The sidewalk and street were strewn with shards of broken glass. For a few minutes the air in the neighborhood was filled with a heaving, booming sound, dull but powerful, as thunder or artillery fire. Then all was quiet again.

Surprisingly, only two people were injured as a result of the destruction. Both were elderly. One was a woman who had been standing in her living room flipping through the *TV Guide* when her window went. She fainted immediately and in falling to the floor gashed her forehead superficially on a corner of the coffee table. The wound looked much worse than it actually was. The other person was a retired milkman who was just about to unlock his car and drive to Waterbury to visit his sister. He heard the sound as the first windows exploded and stood as if hypnotized, car keys in one hand, watching. Even when it reached 127, his own house, he could not move. His face and hands were pitted with small cuts and a large piece of broken plate glass sheared into his left leg just above the knee, almost completely severing it.

Father Lombardy felt silly, sitting on a rock a few yards away from the clearing by himself and with nothing happening. This was the third day of his vigil and he was beginning to wonder if the whole thing wasn't a waste of time. When would it come? In the meantime, what if someone saw him there? It would look peculiar, to say the least Yesterday he had seen a group of school children on the hill, several hundred yards in the distance, but they showed no sign of having spotted him. He had felt even more foolish, crouching uncomfortably lower in the tall grass.

The conversation with Art Pomar had not gone very well. Father Lombardy was unable to work out any coherent or sensible line of explanation and so he had fallen back on the feeble argument that the site was dangerous, and the children should not be allowed to play there or even pass by on their way home from school. Pomar readily agreed to this but he had expected a good deal more from the priest.

"Father, Joey says you saw Her too. Is that right?" The parent's anxiety came through on the phone, loud and clear.

"No, Art, that's not right."

"He lied to me, and about a priest?"

"No, wait a minute, Art. Calm down. Joey didn't lie, not exactly."

"Well, what then, Father?"

"I saw something. We both did. That much is true." Father Lombardy worried the press-buttons on the address pad beside the telephone.

"You did see."

"Something," the priest stressed, wondering if that was hope he heard in Pomar's voice. "It was a cloud of gas or something., I don't know what. Maybe pollution and smoke."

"Oh." Pomar sounded unconvinced.

"But it was most certainly not Our Lady."

"You're sure of that, Father?"

"Absolutely."

After a brief, uneasy silence, Pomar said: "Joey told us She threw you in the air." It sounded like an accusation.

"It was not She," Father Lombardy repeated as forcefully as he could without shouting. "When that cloud settled on us, Art, and it happened pretty suddenly, we jumped and, uh, fell. Then we got out of there as fast as we could. Besides the Virgin Mary doesn't go around throwing people through the air."

"You ran, Father?"

"I told you, Art, whatever it is it isn't healthy. In fact, it's probably dangerous. A pocket of gas from a factory, maybe. If I had been alone that would be one thing, but I wanted to get your boy safely out of there."

Even now, as he sat on the rock, Father Lombardy felt annoyed with himself for twisting his way out of an honest answer. But he was also beginning to think that perhaps he had been right about the cloud. Whatever it was, it had not appeared again. Perhaps the cloud had dispersed in the air, harmlessly. Perhaps he had imagined more than actually happened that day with Joey Pomar. Perhaps he had psyched himself into a state of expectation before the cloud had arrived, and when it did he had over-reacted. Perhaps he only imagined those faces.

But the thought of evil came back to him, and it was much harder to explain away. He had been very upset that night, confused and upset. After a couple of hours out here, waiting for anything, the cloud began to seem less evil and more bizarre. Odd. The kind of thing people write about in the Sunday newspapers. Strange experiences.

Father Lombardy glanced at his watch. He would give it another ten minutes. Sweat trickled down the side of his body.

Click-click.

The priest looked up and saw a fat grey squirrel perched on the rocks above the clearing. The animal worked rapidly on an acorn. Tiny bits of shell dropped through the empty air.

Over breakfast that morning Father Connors had seemed to make a point of not asking about the Pomar children. Father Lombardy didn't want to talk about it but felt obliged to say something. Eventually he had asked, "What if the children did see—something?"

"The last thing we want to do is give the Protestants reason to think we're reverting to the Middle Ages," Father Connors had replied drily.

———

Ed Tuttle dropped an empty paper cup into the waste basket on his way out of the office. He was a librarian, and it was closing time at the Millville Public Library. Alison Maxwell, the young lady he had employed a few months ago, was date-stamping books for someone. Ed glanced into the magazine reading-room, found it empty as expected, and then walked to the front desk.

"Can I drop you anywhere, Alison?"

"No, thanks, Mr. Tuttle. I have to clean up a few things here and then stop at the supermarket on my way home." She spoke in the same firm but friendly tone of voice she used at least three nights a week when Ed Tuttle offered her a ride. She knew she was neither especially pretty nor a flashy dresser but that didn't seem to bother Ed Tuttle, who eyed her appreciatively at every available opportunity. She didn't mind; he wasn't pushy.

"See you tomorrow," Tuttle said, wearing his smile of resignation. He waved as he walked to the door.

"Good night."

She went back to the book she was reading, *Car* by Harry Crews, a novel about a man who tries to eat an automobile. She had one more page to the end of the chapter and she wanted to finish it before leaving.

Alison Maxwell was twenty-two. She had graduated from Boston University a semester early but, to the chagrin of her teachers and family, she had decided not to go on for a master's degree, at least not for the time being. She wanted to take some time off, perhaps a year, so she had returned home for a vacation. When the job at the library came up, that settled the matter. It was easy, undemanding work, leaving her plenty of time and energy to pursue anything else that took her interest. Now, a little over four months into the job, she was beginning to have second thoughts. It was too quiet, too relaxed here. Perhaps when the hot summer was over she would be ready to go back to Cambridge. It was a lively place and she needed things to respond to. Millville, by contrast, was a non-event. Pleasant, like inertia, but only in controlled doses.

Alison had not even finished the chapter of *Car* when she heard the noise from the far end of the main library wing. It was a dull clunking noise, quiet but unmistakable. Books were falling on the floor. Must be someone still here, she thought, putting her book away and rising from behind the front desk. When she reached the room the noise was louder, though still muffled by the thick carpeting on the floor. Then she heard a heavy clomping sound, as if a number of people were running up and down the aisles. Alison saw a couple of books fly over a shelf unit and she stopped immediately. Vandals?

She hurried back to the front desk and picked up the phone to buzz Mr. Balinski, the janitor, in the basement. But even as she was dialing he came around the corner from the stairs.

"Evening, miss," he said with a genial smile.

"Mr. Balinski," she said, "thank God you're here."

"What is it?"

"Someone is in there throwing books around."

"Oh are they?" He strode into the main wing and Alison followed closely behind.

They found hundreds of books scattered about on the floor with pages torn out and bindings destroyed. The noise had stopped.

"Oh my God," she exclaimed. "Look at all this."

Mr. Balinski had a quick look around and returned to the girl.

"Nobody here now."

"It's the mayor's office on the line, Chief," the police department switchboard operator said.

"Oh hell." Sturdevent exhaled loudly.

"Want me to tell them you're out?"

"No, that's all right, Betty, I'll take it."

"Okay, Chief. Putting you through."

Sturdevent pulled his memo pad in front of him on the desk as the telephone clicks sounded in his ears.

"Chief Sturdevent?"

"Morning, Mayor. How are you?"

"Not very well."

"I'm sorry to hear that."

"What exactly is going on?"

"With what, Mayor?" As if I don't know, Sturdevent thought grimly. Mayor James D. Sherwin sounded frosty.

"With everything in this town. People have been telling me about a destroyed car, flashing lights, trouble at the library, broken windows and God only knows what else."

"Yes, sir."

"I'd like to know what's going on."

"We've looked into all of these things as they happened, but so far we just haven't been able to come up with anything concrete. I expect it's a small gang of kids causing all the trouble."

"Then why can't your people find them and put a stop to this business?"

"That's what we're trying to do, Major, but we haven't even had a single description to go on. Nobody has seen a thing. Whoever is doing these things has been damn fast"

"From what I've heard there may not even be any vandals involved. The witnesses on Church Street said the windows broke by themselves. What do you know about that?"

"I never heard of a bunch of windows just breaking by themselves, Mayor, but I guess it's possible. You know we think some kind of freak wind might have killed that fellow Donner. If it was, I guess the wind could still be blowing around and causing damage. Though I don't know how it could have gotten inside the library. That building is all shut up all the time because of the air-conditioning system. As for the flashing lights, we've had all sorts of phone calls about them. Red lights, blue lights, green lights, flying saucers—you name it, we got it. Again, it could be some strange thing with the weather, I don't know. Personally, I think some of these people have been staying out in the sun too long."

"Well, I want some answers, Chief."

"Yes, sir."

"This situation is getting out of hand."

"Yes, sir." Christ, who put the bug up Sherwin's ass?

"Have you seen the editorial in this morning's *News*?"

"I haven't had time to read the newspaper yet," Sturdevent replied, pleased with himself for getting in the dig.

"Well, they're asking questions about all these incidents, suggesting they're connected and that the town isn't doing anything about it."

"That's just speculation. They have nothing better to complain about, is all."

Sherwin ignored that. "When they say "the town" they should be saying the police department, because it's a police matter. But they make it sound like the mayor's office, and that's not right."

"No, sir." Did I vote for this asshole?

"Now I'm getting flak because of it"

"I'm sorry about that, but we are doing all we can to get to the bottom of the matter."

"Do they know something we don't know?"

"Nobody does," Sturdevent said.

"What's the situation on that Donner death?"

"It's an open case in our files, but there's not much more we can do about it unless some new evidence turns up."

"I don't like that, Chief."

"No, sir, neither do I." What am I supposed to do, manufacture evidence?

"People just don't die like that, and certainly not in a town like this."

"No, sir."

"Call me by Friday and let me know what you've learned by then."

"Will do." Sturdevent scrawled a note on the pad.

After a pause Mayor Sherwin said, "Sorry if I sound angry with you, Al, that's not the case."

"No problem, Mayor."

"When you hear a few things from friends... and then this editorial..."

"I understand." Sherwin always backs down a step or two, Sturdevent thought.

"Well, call me on Friday."

"Yes, sir."

Sturdevent hung up the telephone and stared at his memo pad for a few moments. Sherwin was a nervous creep, but he was the man in the mayor's seat. Every time he heard something out at the country club he started worrying, and when he worried he had to phone somebody up and make a pest of himself. Hadn't he phoned the town maintenance department about a stop sign that had been knocked slightly out of kilter by a drunk driver once? What the hell kind of mayor was that? Sturdevent would go into politics himself if it weren't for the fact that he'd have to deal with even more of those creeps.

Martin Lasker knew immediately that it wasn't going to be a wasted trip—at least not entirely. Marge Calder had terrific legs and they were very much in evidence as she wore her tight white shorts. Above them she had on a plain yellow shirt. Her hair was cut short around her bright, well-scrubbed face. When she opened the door she looked almost as surprised as Lasker did. Evidently she had been expecting some dogged-looking reporter past forty, perhaps with a fedora pushed back on his head and a grubby cigarette stub pasted into one corner of his mouth. Lasker expected to find a blue-rinse specimen, slightly scatter-brained. Instead, here he was sitting on a back patio, admiring the view and sipping lemonade with a very pleasant young woman.

"So you see," she was saying, "I don't have any axe to grind about flying saucers, one way or the other. I don't believe in them, really, but I don't disbelieve in them either."

"Sure, but you think you've seen them?"

"I saw something, yes. I said they might be flying saucers but I'm not sure. For one thing, they didn't move."

"You saw more than one of them?" Flying saucers that didn't move. Okay, lady.

"Yes, oh, I saw two of them. For three or four nights, on and off, not regularly. Some nights they're there and other nights they're not."

"I see." It sounded decidedly unpromising to Lasker.

"My husband saw them too."

"What does he think they are?"

"Neon signs." Marge Calder made a face.

"I take it you disagree?"

"Yes. For one thing, I drove all around the area, both areas in fact, and there was nothing at all that could be what we saw."

"What exactly did they look like?" Lasker poised his pencil over the pad.

"Bright blue and kind of oval shaped, but an oval standing on its end. Like a very fat cigar." She formed a figure in the air with her hands to indicate what she meant. "Sometimes the blue was almost purple, or maroon."

"And it didn't move at all, you say?"

"Neither of them did. They just kind of sat there, or hovered. What does that sound like to you?"

"A big neon sign." He smiled.

"Aw no, I told you—"

"I don't know what it sounds like, honestly. They may well have been flying saucers, or cigars. You saw them, I didn't."

"You think I'm another dizzy housewife with—"

"No, I don't think that at all. I'm just taking down your story. That's all I can do."

"My neighbor, Sylvia, saw it too."

"She did?"

"Yes, the first time. We were out here talking—"

"At night?"

"No, this was during the afternoon. The first time."

"Really? You must have been able to see it much better in the daylight then."

"Well…" A perplexed look wrinkled across Marge's face. "Not really. It looked just the same, like a blue fire."

"Fire?" Lasker was writing more than he expected.

"Yes, light or fire, that kind of thing."

"What's your neighbor's name?"

"Sylvia Berkowitz. She lives in that house there. I saw her drive away about an hour ago, probably gone shopping before her kids come home from school. But you can get her later, or phone."

"Okay. Anybody else see them besides her and your husband?"

"Not that I know of," she answered. "And don't bother asking my husband because I told you what he thinks. He's a good guy, but he has a closed mind in some respects."

"Okay." The unnecessary personal comment didn't escape Lasker. It wasn't the first one she had volunteered in the twenty minutes they had been talking.

"Are you going to write all this up?"

Lasker finished his lemonade before answering. "Even if I accepted all you have to say at face value, which I'm still not sure I do, I'd have to persuade my editor it was worth running, and that's not an easy thing to do. He's a good old-fashioned newspaperman."

"I thought so."

"What? That we wouldn't write anything?"

"Yes."

"Why are you anxious that we should?"

"I'm not a publicity-seeker, if that's what you mean. In fact, I'd rather have my name left out—my husband wouldn't be too thrilled to find his wife in the paper as having seen flying saucers. But if you wrote something about it, not naming names, you might find that other people would come forth, other people who might have seen something."

"Or a bunch of people—" Lasker carefully avoided the word "cranks"—"who imagine they see something because of what they read in the paper."

"Oh, yeah," Marge said dispiritedly.

"Would you point out where you saw these lights? Where exactly were they?"

"Sure." She stood and pointed across the valley. "See that bit of road that goes up the far side of the valley?"

"Just a little way above that yellow building?"

"Yes, but they're actually about a mile apart. I drove it."

"I know. Yeah, I see the spot."

"That's one, though I'm sure it was up in the air, so it could be anywhere on that line of vision, but far, way over on that side."

"Okay."

"And the other was up there," she said, turning to the north. "I'm not so sure about exactly where it was, because I only saw that one at night."

"Okay, good enough."

Lasker made another note in his pad because he felt compelled to act like a reporter. She was so serious that he did believe she had seen something. Besides, if she was making it up she would at least have had the lights moving or flashing.

"Oh," Lasker suddenly said, stopping as they walked back to the house.

"Nothing," he replied, recovering quickly. A word had belatedly clicked in his mind. She had used the word 'fire' when talking about the sight earlier and Bondarevsky had mentioned swamp-fire to him. Could the two be connected? Could they be the same thing? Swamp-fire, or something else altogether?

As he drove back to the office Lasker was sure he had been given another tiny bit of information that belonged to, but didn't yet fit in with, all the other loose ends he seemed to be collecting.

Lynn Richter flipped through the pages of the expensive magazine, looking briefly at the color photographs of naked people, mostly women. Occasionally she read a few lines of the short accompanying texts, but they seemed silly. She dropped the magazine on the floor and picked up another. Her husband, Hal, was making odd noises in the bathroom. Like most of the people in the photographs, Lynn had no clothes on. She sat on the round, soft hassock in the living room of their modem apartment. They spent a good deal of money on erotic accoutrements. Perhaps too much, she thought, tossing aside the magazine and taking up yet another. It featured a number of women with various animals.

Hal walked into the room carrying several jars, tubes, and more magazines. With his clothes off he looked chubby rather than stout, but that only made him seem more cuddly to Lynn.

"Does this stuff turn you on, Hal?"

"Sometimes," he answered, glancing over her shoulder,

"It doesn't do much for me."

"It's all part of the experience, honey." He dropped everything he was holding on the couch. It was a plain black Naugahyde-upholstered piece of furniture, but the Richters had bought an imitation leopard-skin coverlet for it.

"What about animals?" Lynn held up a photograph of a young woman fella ting an Alsatian. The woman seemed to be smiling, which made the picture seem even stranger to Lynn.

"Bestiality, no..." Hal said, studying the page: "Not personally, that is. But it can be interesting in the historical sense. Remember Leda and the swan? And the Romans used to get up to the darnedest things with animals, and it's all fact." Hal was working on a Ph.D. in history. Once every week or two he drove to the University of Connecticut at Storrs to meet with his professor or continue his research at the library.

"It doesn't do anything for me." Lynn looked through the other magazines on the floor.

"You have to approach these things with an open mind, honey." Hal picked up the magazine Lynn had dropped, *Animal Farm*.

"I do have an open mind. I told you."

"I know," Hal said, distracted.

"It just doesn't do much for me."

"That's okay."

"It is?"

"Sure. The important thing is to have an open mind on the subject. Keep your lines clear."

"Well, I do, but I don't see the point of all these magazines if they don't do anything for me."

"You like the films though." Hal continued to speak in the same distracted tone of voice as he peered intently at the photographs. He was looking at a sequence featuring a woman and a horse. Old hat, he thought.

"The films are okay, some of them. The ones that don't jump all over the place."

"Yeah."

"But they're so expensive, Hal."

"Yeah. Why don't you play with the vibrator?"

Lynn sighed histrionically. He was always telling her to play with the vibrator. "I don't want to."

"How come?"

"I feel silly."

"That's silly."

"What is?"

"Feeling silly."

"I can't help it."

"You're supposed to enjoy it."

"How can I enjoy it if I don't enjoy it?"

"You want to be self-aware, not just self-conscious. Explore yourself." Hal put down the magazine and picked up a paperback book.

Lynn was examining the personal aids at the back of a journal called *Hypermodern Sexology*. "Some of these people," she said, more to herself than Hal.

Hal had found a passage in the paperback. "Here you are, Lynn." He began to read aloud: ""*Now you can see why her legs had to be apart, and reasonably free to move—so that she can give herself some sort of*"—blank "*action when she moves, as she will, when she feels the whip across her ass and tits.*" Got that? "*Some sort of*—blank—*action.*" What do you think it is, honey?"

"I don't know."

"Come on, Lynn, guess."

"Fucking?"

"Nope."

"Screwing? I don't know."

"Wanking."

"What's that?" Lynn looked more annoyed than puzzled.

"That's British for masturbating."

"Oh." Things like that always fascinated Hal.

"Incredible," Hal murmured, reading on silently.

"I never cared for that game much. It turns me on more when I read to myself. Not out loud."

"Listen—"

"Oh, Hal."

Lynn launched herself from the hassock, tackling her husband and tumbling onto the couch with him, and then onto the floor.

"What the hell—" Hal exclaimed.

"Come on, lover," Lynn whispered urgently, kissing him and biting him playfully around his ears and neck.

"Just a minute." Hal struggled to get free but Lynn had him in a firm neck-lock.

"Now you're ready, now."

"Let me get the cream, honey."

"Never mind the cream."

"Never mind the cream?" Hal sounded outraged. "You know I always come too fast. Come on, let go."

"Damn you." Lynn released him. That Hal could be so coldblooded and erect at the same time always amazed her. She watched him hop across the floor, open the jar of Slo Fun and calmly begin to apply the pasty white unguent.

"Oooh," he said.

"I should have made an appointment."

"You're not helping matters, Lynn."

"Does that?"

"Wait and see." Hal spun around, more eager than ever, presenting a large shiny white sight that Lynn was careful not to smile at. "Vait und zee." He began to crawl towards his wife.

Lynn grabbed a handful of paperbacks from the floor and threw them at Hal. "Stay away, you robot." Hal ignored the books, snarling and advancing. "I said stay away." Lynn backed toward the French-

style doors that opened out onto their small balcony. From the side
table by Hal's easy chair she picked up a Readers Digest volume of
condensed novels and hurled it forcefully at her approaching husband,
but he knocked it aside and jumped for her. Lynn stepped further back
but Hal caught one of her ankles, pulling her to the floor. He half-stood
and began dragging her across the carpet. Lynn moaned and
whimpered audibly, responding more to the part now. Hal rolled her
over onto her stomach and sat on her ass, pinning her arms beneath his
knees. With one hand he gently grabbed her chin and pulled her head
slightly up and back on her neck, holding her there. With the other
hand he picked up the vibrator, deftly switched it on and forced it into
Lynn's mouth. It clattered against her teeth. She resisted it at first but
quickly accepted the humming, plastic phallus. Only then did he
stretch out, force her legs apart and enter her from behind.

He came within thirty seconds, setting off a chain of curses directed
at the not-so-Slo Fun, but he kept on pumping for another minute. Then
he was so soft it was impossible to stay in her, and anyhow Lynn's cries
had subsided. They rolled a few inches apart and Hal switched off the
vibrator.

"You're so big," Lynn said in her little-girl voice, pressing the side
of her face against his chest. Hal smiled down at her but said nothing.
His heart still boomed. Too goddamn fast, but fun, he thought. In a few
minutes Lynn's even breathing told him she had dozed off, and he shut
his own eyes.

Hal had nearly fallen asleep himself when the bright light filled the
room. He started to open his eyes, but a coherent thought never formed
in his mind. They were lifted from the shag carpet in a rush. Everything
in the room seemed to be moving. A modular, stainless steel vase
crushed in the back half of Hal's skull.

Lynn didn't even wake from her slumber. She was thrown against
one corner of the mantel over their non-functional fireplace. One of her
carotid arteries was torn open and she died instantly.

It was over in seconds.

"Nice apartment," Ned Hanley said, looking around cheerfully and almost making a point of ignoring the bodies on the floor. "What do you think—four hundred a month?"

"Not much damage done," Sturdevent remarked. "Not much damage at all. Compared to the other one."

"I'd say three to four hundred. Look at this place. Nice furniture, nice layout. If he was a student and she worked in the bank, how the hell could they afford it?" Hanley swept the palm of one hand across an expanse of wall 'Jesus, even the wallpaper is like a rug. Feel that."

Sturdevent knelt beside the body of Lynn Richter. "Nice-looking girl. Husband's a little pudgy, but they were a nice-looking couple."

"Yeah," Hanley sneered, poking through the magazines on the floor.

"But it doesn't seem to fit in with Donner."

"Look at all this stuff," Hanley said, prodding the litter. "I didn't know you needed so much equipment to get laid."

"Fun and games," Sturdevent said evenly.

"Yeah, shit." Hanley sounded disgusted.

"Heritage House Apartments," Sturdevent said to himself, rising. Hanley seemed to resent the people living here. He nosed around like a voyeur getting a glimpse of some previously forbidden territory. But Sturdevent felt only tired and heartsick. Not so much for the dead couple before him, but because their deaths meant trouble, big trouble. There would be trouble with the newspapers, trouble with Town Hall. And, worst of all, more trouble from whoever or whatever was causing all this death and destruction.

"I'll tell you one thing," Hanley said, coming across the room to where Sturdevent stood.

"What's that?"

"This looks to me like murder. Plain and simple."

"Thanks a lot," Sturdevent said drily. "What else is new?"

"No, I mean, you can't blame this on a freak wind." Sturdevent looked at him sharply, anger in his eyes, but Hanley continued. "Look, there's stuff ripped and broken and scattered around, but not like the last time. Not nearly as bad as the last time."

"Yeah." The Chief glanced at his watch. "Where are those guys anyhow? They should be here by now, going over everything." He didn't want to admit that he agreed with Hanley. This did look like nothing more than a nasty, dirty little double murder. And that threw the Donner case into question again. It's not going to... die down, he thought.

"They'll be here," Hanley said evenly. "Have you thought about putting up roadblocks?"

"For who?" Sturdevent's anger brimmed. Only yesterday he welcomed suggestions. Now they were an unwanted intrusion. "We don't know who we're looking for? It's too damn late, anyhow."

"I suppose so. If you ask me, these people got up to some kinky stuff. Regularly, from the looks of it. Maybe with other couples or another person. Threesomes are quite popular, I hear."

"Yeah, where'd you hear that?"

"*Time* Magazine," Hanley shot back quickly.

"A sex killing." Sturdevent snorted. It didn't seem likely. Nothing seemed likely. What the hell was going on in this town? "Check the kitchen and bathroom for dope."

"I already did, before you arrived. Nothing. Nothing disturbed in the other rooms, either. I don't know if anything's missing, but I wouldn't bet on a robbery that got out of hand. Not in the circumstances."

Sturdevent decided he didn't want to listen to any more of Hanley's talk. Hanley seemed almost happy that this double murder had taken place. Maybe he thinks that if things get bad enough in this town I'll be relieved of my position. Unsolved: rampant vandalism, three deaths. Hanley would love it. Not that he could do any better at figuring it all out. Screw him, the Mayor, the newspaper. And yet I'm the one on the spot It's between me and this—person or persons unknown. Or thing. This isn't a big-city police force; they'll look to me, not to my juniors. They don't shake up the ranks in a small town. Just roll a head, get another one.

"I want everything on these two people by eleven-thirty tomorrow morning, Ned."

"Yeah."

"Everything. I mean it. I want to know more about these people than they knew about themselves."

"Yeah."

"I don't care if you have to take Dingus off parking tickets. Use everybody you need and don't sleep on it."

"Okay," Hanley said, mildly surprised. Dingus was the dumbest man in three counties. After twelve years on the force he still had trouble filling out parking tickets correctly. He would go into a restaurant and order Soup-in-a-Basket, so the story went. Sturdevent's feeling desperate, Hanley thought.

"I'm going." Sturdevent started for the door.

"Home?"

Sturdevent didn't answer. Let Hanley wonder about it. A police chief shouldn't hang around like any other cop. That's part of the trouble, being too much one of the boys. It didn't pay, not with someone like Hanley.

In the hallway outside the Richters' apartment, a small crowd of people had gathered. Corwin stood near the door, talking to the caretaker, jotting down notes. The other people, residents of Heritage House, clustered a few yards away. Sturdevent took Corwin aside for a moment.

"You get anything yet?" the Chief asked quietly.

"Nothing that sounds very helpful, Chief."

"Hunh, figures."

"Everybody seemed to like the Richters and—"

"Keep on it." Sturdevent walked toward the exit.

"Chief?"

Someone placed a hand on Sturdevent's arm. It was Martin Lasker. Sturdevent continued walking.

"Chief, any chance I can get in the apartment for a look around?"

"Nope. Nobody gets in there unless they're on official police business." Sturdevent punched the heat-sensitive elevator call-button. He had to hit it a second time before it connected.

"Mind if I ask you a few questions about it?"

Sturdevent looked at the reporter. Lasker had his portable cassette. The reels were spinning slowly. The Chief turned to the elevator, waiting impatiently for it to arrive. Expensive place like this should have fast lifts.

"You want me to turn this off?" Lasker pushed a button on the recorder and shoved the microphone in his jacket pocket. "It's off, Chief."

The elevator rumbled open and both men stepped inside.

"What'd you want to go and run that damn editorial for the other day?"

"It wasn't my idea," Lasker answered, trying to recover from the unexpected jab, but sounding only defensive. "I have to tell Phipps everything I'm working on—that's just routine. I didn't even have enough for him to okay a news story, but he went and wrote that leader. It surprised me too, Chief, honest."

"You got a lot to learn about the newspaper business, Martin. About business, period."

"Well—"

"For one thing you got me and a lot of other folks annoyed, for no good reason. For another thing, you let that guy steal your story, even if it wasn't ready yet. He got in with it first."

Lasker grimaced as they emerged from the elevator in the ground-floor lobby. Maybe Sturdevent was right, but there were two dead people up on the fourth floor and that was what Lasker wanted to talk about now. More people stood around in the lobby and on the front walk. Lasker waited until they were alone again in the parking lot around back.

"What happened upstairs?"

"Two people were killed, but I'm sure you know that already, Martin."

"The same way Donner died?"

"No."

"No?" Lasker was startled.

"No, not at all like the Donner case, Martin." The Chief made a point of speaking Lasker's first name clearly and firmly, like a father lecturing a child.

"Well, how did they die?"

"You'll have to wait for the official report, Martin, same as me." Sturdevent got into his car and switched on the ignition.

"Mind if I ride with you, Chief?"

"I'm going the other way, Martin. Sorry."

Sturdevent began to back out of his parking space.

"Hang on, Chief, I'm not going anywhere special. Which way are you heading?"

The police car roared off. Lasker watched it disappear from sight, and then he started walking back to the apartment building. He was annoyed with Sturdevent, but even more annoyed with himself.

CHAPTER SEVEN

Lasker had just finished typing out his short report on the deaths at Heritage House Apartments. He read through it quickly, making occasional corrections in pencil. Eight paragraphs that said very little: the bare police statement, a few details about who the Richters were and what they did, a couple of comments from neighbors, and not much else. Tony Baker had taken a good photograph of the scene in the corridor outside the Richters' apartment It showed policeman Corwin looking harassed, which was perhaps a bit unfair, but it would make a nice front-page splash.

Lasker picked up his three sheets of yellow copy-paper and took them into Phipps' office.

The editor was considering various possible headlines; five or six candidates were printed in block letters on scraps of proof paper on his desk.

"Thanks, Marty," Phipps said, taking Lasker's copy. "I'll finish this up if it needs anything. You can head for home now."

"I'll stay, if you think you'll need me."

"That's okay. Get some sleep. I'll want you camping on the front step of the police department tomorrow morning, and you've already had a long day today." Phipps rearranged the headlines on his desk.

"I like that one," Lasker said, placing a finger on the headline which struck him as being least sensational.

Phipps grunted.

"Okay, good night."

"Night, Marty."

Lasker strolled lazily back to his desk. He did feel tired, now that he thought about it. It always amazed him how Phipps, who was getting on in years, had so much energy and stamina. He remained at the office to put the paper to bed almost every night, even when the most exciting news was nothing more than a rainstorm washing out some garden fete. And he was generous—Phipps might completely rewrite some of the copy Lasker handed in, but he wouldn't touch the by-line. That editorial seemed to be a strange quirk, but Lasker was inclined to believe that Phipps knew what he was doing. A good old country newspaperman. The kind Lasker thought he would like to become.

"Marty!"

Lasker had just picked up his jacket when he heard the familiar voice call his name. He turned and saw Dave Lutz standing in the doorway of the newsroom. He looked out of breath.

"Hi," Lasker said, walking over to him. "What are you doing here. It's—almost eleven."

"I tried your place, and then took a chance I'd find you here."

"You just did. I'm leaving."

"Good. Now," Lutz was still catching his breath. Sweat dripped down his face.

"What's up?"

"I've seen them."

"What? Who?" But Lasker was immediately sure he knew what Lutz was talking about.

"Three figures, whatever they are. They looked like they were on fire, a whitish glow. Like ghosts, but fiery. Come on, I want to take you back and see if they're still there."

"Where?" the reporter asked, following Lutz who was already out the door and on his way down the stairs.

"Out in the meadows, where they're planning to build that new airport"

"What were you doing out there?" They had reached Lutz's beat-up old Volvo. "That's out in the middle of nowhere."

"I know," Lutz. "I was taking Sandy home. You don't know what I gave up to come and find you."

"Sandy who?"

"You don't know her. Nice girl. This was less than an hour ago. We must have been only about a quarter of a mile away from them. They were very bright and just walking around in the field. Very slowly, like a kind of ghostly procession. Christ, I never saw anything like it. I'm a believer now, though I'm not sure in what." The words tumbled out of Lutz's mouth.

"You saw them in a field?" Lasker felt stupid and slow. The heat, even at this hour of the night, was a shock after the air-conditioned office. He was also distracted by the idea that Lutz might actually be involved with one of his students—something he said he would never do.

"Yeah, meadow, field. There were trees around, toward the far end, near where they were. Yeah, it was at the edge of the meadow."

"Tell me again what they looked like to you."

"Like a hole had opened up in the ground and these three things beamed out arid started moving around. Bright. Like a fire flickering and sparking in a breeze. We watched them for, oh, I don't know, fifteen minutes maybe. Then I dropped Sandy off home and came looking for you. Let me tell you, that's friendship."

"You think they were ghosts?"

"Shit, I don't know what they were." Lutz pulled a half bottle of vodka out of the glove compartment, unscrewed the cap using his teeth and took a large gulp. "Try this," he said, passing the container to Lasker.

"Thanks," the reporter said dubiously.

"They weren't ordinary people, that's for sure," Lutz went on. "And they weren't the Ku Klux Klan either."

Lasker thought about it. He didn't believe in ghosts but he didn't disbelieve either—like Marge Calder, he realized. He knew Lutz to be completely reliable, even when he had been drinking.

"I called Bondarevsky today, hoping he might have seen his swamp-fire again, but he said no."

"Who's Bondarevsky?"

"The guy whose cow got killed. Remember? I told you about it."

"Students are supposed to remember, man. Us teachers keep trying to forget."

The car bounced along a back road now, rattling and grinding at every little dip and bend. The rush of air was refreshing.

"This is like the Hardy boys," Lutz said with a grin.

"You're going to destroy this car," Lasker replied, bracing his feet and holding firmly onto the door.

"It already has a hundred and twenty-three thousand miles on the clock. What more do you want?"

"To get there alive."

"What were you doing at the office so late anyway?"

Lasker quickly told his friend about the events at Heritage House. Lutz said nothing throughout, but Lasker could see that the teacher's eyes were wide and alert in the pale glow of the dash-board lights. Lasker omitted the short, unhappy conversation he had had with Sturdevent.

"God, it sounds more and more sinister," Lutz said when Lasker had finished.

"Yeah, but apparently it wasn't as messy as the other guy, Donner. They're talking about it as a straightforward sex murder, if there is such a thing."

"We're almost there now."

The country road ribboned out onto a broad, flat plain. Somewhere out there, Lasker thought, they're going to stick up an airport. A small regional airport, mostly to handle cargo. But it'd be big enough to take some jets, and there was already talk of a passenger shuttle-service to New York and Boston. In a few years there will be nothing but concrete over all this—of course, a highway will have to swing through. What good is an airport without easy access to a highway? The thought of it all made Martin Lasker even more depressed as he looked out the car window across the expanse of open earth.

"Here. We were stopped just along here, I think it was." Lutz pulled over to the edge of the road and onto a grassy shoulder. A low barbed-wire fence ran along the border of the field, partially obscured by a fringe of tall weeds and brambles. The meadows rolled away on both sides of the road for hundreds of yards. In the distance a dark wall of trees could be discerned against the night skyline.

"Who owns all this land out here?" Lutz asked, getting out of the car and looking around.

"I think it belongs to the Mason family, or a lot of it does. But they live most of the year in Florida. Lots of money in that family."

"Right."

Lasker came around to where Lutz stood by the fence. "Where exactly did you see them?" It was becoming a familiar question with him.

"Straight out there." Lutz pointed.

"You don't see them now, do you?"

"Smart-ass."

"Let's take a look."

Lasker stepped carefully over the rusty barbed-wire and set off across the field. Lutz caught up with him and a few minutes later they stood within thirty yards of the woods. All around them the blanket of field grass and wild flowers had been gouged and ripped up, leaving great jagged scars of bare soil about eight inches deep. The damage was unmistakable, even in the poor night light. Both men stood staring for several moments in silence. Lasker felt an uneasy calm settle over him. Yes, it had been here all right. He was sure of it. Who would come out here and do this? Murderers? Vandals? Animal killers? Ghosts? Flying saucers? It? They? The wind? What tied everything together? What link? Why couldn't he put his finger on it?

In the night air, slowly cooling, there was no breeze.

It wouldn't do.

Sturdevent thumbed through the fat stack of notes, photocopies and documents that made up Ned Hanley's instant file on the Richters. Of course he had received everything on the dead couple; everything and nothing. There was no indication that they had fooled around sexually with other people and that was what Sturdevent had hoped to find. They had no money problems (his family provided a discreet academic subsidy while Hal Richter worked on his thesis) and they had no known enemies. An intelligent young man. An attractive young woman. A handsome couple. With prospects. Unfortunately dead.

Doc Schmidt's preliminary report wasn't much help either. The man had been killed with the steel vase (as Sturdevent suspected) and the woman had been killed on the corner of the mantel (as Sturdevent had feared). Although the room was comparatively undisturbed the case was wide open, and could easily be related to the Donner case. It had to be. That feeling was closing in on Sturdevent again.

But he still wanted to believe it was a clear-cut murder, nothing more. Perhaps Donner had been murdered too—but that was a can of worms he didn't want to re-open, at least not until he had to. Donner was a nobody, a pale grey bachelor clerk tending towards total invisibility. Sure, people talked about it some and wondered. It was a little odd, no doubt about it. But the matter of his death had faded quickly and without any real difficulty. Nobody could get too worked up about a guy like Donner.

Unfortunately, it would be quite a different matter with the Richters. They were young, which always counts for more with some people. There were two of them and one was a woman, which really made things a lot worse. And they were good-looking. And they had friends. And there would be a stink this time. And Sturdevent was more depressed than ever.

He had suckered himself with Hanley, too. That son of a bitch *had* worked all night on the Richter file, with three other members of the force. They had rung bells, pounded on doors, slammed brass knockers until at least four in the morning, talking to friends and even casual acquaintances of Hal and Lynn Richter. Waking people up, grilling them in the middle of the night practically until dawn... The desk already had half a dozen complaints and the leaden feeling in Sturdevent's gut told him it wouldn't stop there. Hanley was now home sleeping like a babe. He could dump crap on Hanley about it but he knew that wouldn't do any good. Hanley would just shrug and say he was carrying out Sturdevent's orders. Sooner or later, probably much sooner, one of those irate citizens will be in touch with the mayor's office and when that happens Sherwin will be in here shitting ping pong balls all over the place, he thought. He'll be steamed up about these two deaths as it is. Nice new apartment complex, and all that. Sturdevent wondered glumly why the mayor hadn't been on the phone to him already.

He looked at his watch. Twelve-ten. He looked at the sludgy remains in the bottom of his coffee-cup. Shouldn't drink so much of that crap, especially in this weather. Next thing, the doctor'll tell me my blood pressure is doing a permanent rhumba.

He looked at his desk. It was a nice, neat desk, well-ordered and with few papers on it. The kind of desk that said not much was happening around here. Which was usually the case.

Sturdevent began writing on his memo pad. He drew up a list much the same as the one Martin Lasker was keeping, but shorter, starting with cow and ending with Richters. What did it all mean? This town... my town...

Too much brooding, Sturdevent thought abruptly. There are things to do, even if they prove to be of little help. He picked up the telephone and rang through to the basement. After several minutes' delay, which annoyed the Chief, someone answered.

"Anything in on the telex from Hartford yet?"

"Nothing, Chief."

"I want it on my desk before the ink dries."

"I have a note on that, Chief."

Sturdevent hung up. When it did arrive, the State's list of known sex-offenders, murderers, manslaughter cases, assault-and-battery cons and anyone else remotely similar, would give his people something more to get busy with, but he didn't expect anything significant to come of it. Go through the motions.

Hell, the Richter case wasn't even a genuine sex crime. They'd screwed, yeah, but each other.

Sturdevent shook himself, as if physically to break loose from his gloom, and rose from his desk. He would go home and have lunch. His wife would cheer him up and get him ready for the next round. He wouldn't even have to answer the phone if the Mayor called. Fed and refreshed, he would return to the office and jump up and down on Hanley. Just for the hell of it.

Then maybe figure some new angle of approach on these killings. There's got to be a handle somewhere and I'll find it. Some basic point. Maybe they ought to look more closely into the State mental-health records on people in this area.

Something.

Father Lombardy knew that some people thought highly of Peter Demianovich Ouspensky, but after a difficult half-hour of reading *Tertium Organum* the young priest was ready to give up. He had struggled on into the fifth chapter, but it seemed a fruitless, misguided exercise. Ouspensky was an ambitious but muddled thinker, and Father Lombardy was beginning to feel he had been silly to be persuaded to take the book from the library by its subtitle: "A Key to the Enigmas of the World." So far the Russian had succeeded at nothing but being mildly provocative, and even then he was still confusing.

"It is possible that four-dimensional space is the distance between a group of solids, separating these solids, yet at the same time binding them into some to us inconceivable whole, even though they seem to be separate from one another." Ouspensky apparently thought that to be of some importance as he repeated the idea with variations several times thereafter. But Father Lombardy couldn't follow it.

And again:

"We may conceive of the three-dimensional bodies of our space somewhat in the nature of images in our space of to us incomprehensible four-dimensional bodies."

It would be easier to believe in ghosts and demons than to get snarled up in all this mystical chic, Father Lombardy thought, as he tossed the heavy book onto his desk. Why had he even bothered to look at it? To prove he was open-minded? A waste of time. No, it was something else—a way of avoiding the sense of fear that had started growing like a seed in his mind that first day with Joey Pomar. He hadn't seen the apparition again, but it was no less real to him.

Father Lombardy lit a cigarette.

There's good reason to worry, he thought, as if trying to persuade himself anew. He had read about the terrible deaths in the apartment building the other day, and about other strange things that had been happening in town lately. He was sure they were related in some way to the evil presence he had encountered. But how? And, more importantly, what was it? There was of course every chance that it could, and would ultimately, be explained according to the laws of science and man. But it was equally possible that all such explanations would fail, in which case he would be left with only—*only?*—the supernatural.

Somebody knocked timidly on his door.

"Come in," the priest called.

The door opened a little way and the housekeeper stuck her face a few inches into the room. "Father Connors would like to see you, Father."

"Yes, all right."

"He's in the sitting-room, Father."

"Thank you."

The door clicked shut again. Father Lombardy rose from his chair, went to the sink, splashed water on his face and roughly combed his hair in place with his hands. The pastor probably wanted to discuss something silly, like having the faded white lines in the church parking lot repainted, but Father Lombardy welcomed the distraction. He knew he had spent too much time sitting around and brooding about his riddle.

He felt brighter and bounder when he strode into the ground-floor sitting-room, but that feeling was immediately deflated. Father Connors sat in his ancient leather easy-chair and there were several other people present. Father Lombardy recognized Art Pomar, but none of the others. Clearly a meeting was in progress and Father Lombardy felt uncomfortable in his sports-shirt and slacks. Everyone stood up as he entered, which only seemed to make things worse.

"Father Lombardy," the pastor said. "Sorry to call you in without advance notice." The old priest looked grim but he still managed that sly flicker of a smile.

"That's all right. What is it?"

"I believe you already know Mr. Pomar?"

"Yes, hello."

Art Pomar nodded nervously to Father Lombardy.

"This is Mr. Mikenas," Father Connors continual. "And Mr. Duhl, Mr. Schreiber and Mr. Henderson."

Father Lombardy shook hands with each person in turn, then they all resumed their seats. A citizens' committee, Father Lombardy thought unhappily. Something has happened.

"These gentlemen are here about the sightings of the Virgin Mary that started with Mr. Pomar's children, Father," the pastor explained. He paused for a moment, but it was clear from the stony look on his face that Father Lombardy was not going to say anything quickly, so Father Connors continued. "Since you were involved in this situation from the beginning, I'd be grateful if you would bring us up to date on your own activities and thoughts, Father, before we go any further."

The old priest tried to look kindly and sympathetic but to Father Lombardy he merely looked distressing. The whole gathering seemed distressing. Why was he on the spot? Who were these people and what were they doing here? Was he being set up for something?

"I'm sorry, Father Connors, but I feel like I'm dropping in at the deep end. This meeting has obviously already been in progress before I got here and I'd like to know just what it's all about. Would you please bring *me* up to date?"

"Well, I'm sorry," Father Connors responded immediately. "Of course, it must seem strange to you, coming into a room full of new faces." The pastor paused again as if to let Father Lombardy say yes, but the young priest remained silent. "As I said, these gentlemen are here about the sightings. You may or may not know that there have been several more sightings since you last spoke with Mr. Pomar. Several more," Father Connors repeated.

"I see," Father Lombardy said curtly. His uneasiness shaded into anger now. It *was* going to get out of hand.

"It seems that many children, including the children of all these gentlemen, have now seen the—apparition of Our Lady. They feel, and I quite agree, that something must be done about it. The sooner the better. That's what we are here to discuss. But first, we would like to know what you think. You have had time to look into the matter and think about it."

"Yes, and I've already told Mr. Pomar what I think about this thing. That is, I don't believe it actually is Our Lady. In fact, I'm sure it isn't. I think the whole thing is ridiculous and perhaps even dangerous." Father Lombardy could see mounting concern on the faces of the parents sitting opposite him, but he continued without pausing. "I don't pretend to know what the—thing—is, but I know it is not the

Virgin Mary. I told Mr. Pomar, and I still think it's a plausible theory, that what the children are seeing may be some kind of gas cloud, caused by a pocket of pollution that has simply accumulated and hasn't yet been dispersed by the wind. I felt it, and smelled it, and it's nasty, believe me, which is why I say it may be dangerous. You say there have been many more sightings. If that's true, then it means the cloud is still floating around. And may still be dangerous. I admit it's an unusual sight to see, impressive even. But it is not Mary, the Mother of God, not by any stretch of the imagination. We've had hot, still weather for the last month or so, and it seems most likely to me that this cloud is nothing more than a mass of chemical exhaust from some factory or other. If there had been any wind to speak of, it would have been long gone by now."

Father Lombardy now paused but no one else had anything to say. "That's what it looked like to me and that's what I think." Having said all that, Father Lombardy realized it sounded even more persuasive than he actually believed. But another look at the faces around the room told him his story hadn't fallen on receptive ground. Even Father Connors looked unhappy, as if he had heard pretty much what he expected to hear.

"Mr. Pomar tells us that you were physically thrown through the air by this apparition," the pastor said. Is that right, Father?"

"The cloud descended on us suddenly. We jumped and fell down," Father Lombardy lied with some annoyance. "And in any event, I never heard of Our Lady throwing people around."

"Nor have I heard of a cloud doing that."

Father Lombardy had no reply to the pastor's remark.

The pastor continued: "Did you see this—whatever—only the one time, Father?"

"Yes. I went back to the place four times after the incident, always at the same time of day the children said it appeared. But I never saw it again. In retrospect, I'm sorry I left so quickly the day it was there. I should have stayed and taken a closer look at it, but I was concerned about the safety of Mr. Pomar's son."

"Of course." The pastor fell silent for a few moments, staring at his shoes. "It isn't your fault, Father Lombardy, but I'm afraid what you have had to say isn't very helpful at this stage."

"What do you mean by "this stage"?" Father Lombardy asked tartly. This solemn-faced gathering seemed more and more ludicrous to him, and Father Connors, busy being dignified and magisterial, was lending it a sense of importance it didn't deserve. Not this way.

"Well, you aren't the only adult who has seen—Our Lady. Mr. Duhl and Mr. Henderson here both say they saw Her."

"What? Her?" Father Lombardy was stunned and he knew he wasn't hiding it.

"That's right, Father," Mr. Henderson said. "Don and I both saw Her."

"Where? When?"

"Two nights ago," Henderson said. "We were driving home from Veterans' Field."

"We had taken our boys down to watch a Babe Ruth League game," Duhl put in.

"That's right. We were driving back on the Old Springfield Road, about nine o'clock or so."

"That's right, about nine. It was getting dark."

"In fact," Henderson said, patting his paunch, "it was already pretty dark out on that road. Lots of trees, low in the valley, you know."

"Well, where exactly was—She?" Father Lombardy asked, trying to cut through the extraneous matter.

"In the woods out there," Henderson replied. "Like a great burning figure surrounded by a blue light."

"Surrounded?" Father Lombardy could scarcely believe the word, which seemed to separate the figure from the rest of the apparition.

"That's right," Duhl chimed in. "Surrounded Her like an enormous halo."

"Well, or a cloud, I guess you could say," Henderson added.

Fearing that the two men would get into a full-scale search for the exact word, Father Lombardy pressed on. "Where in the woods? Presumably it wasn't right by the side of the road?"

"Right in the middle of the road, Father," Duhl exclaimed, quite excited now. "Bang in the middle."

"I was driving, Father," Henderson said, trying to assume control of the narrative again. "And as Don says, She was slap in the middle of the road. We came around a bend and there She was about thirty yards or so ahead of us. I wasn't going too fast anyhow, you know what those back roads are like, but I had to break sharp as it was. We stopped about—well, pretty close to Her."

"Close enough to have a perfect view," Duhl said.

"And you saw Our Lady?"

"I swear, Father," Duhl said.

"We talked about it most of the night, Father, because we weren't going to get hysterical about it but, yes, we saw Her. I believe we did. She was right in the center of the light. You could see Her all right. I can understand how you might think it was a gas cloud seeing it briefly and maybe not getting a good look, but we saw it close up and clearly, and it was Her, Father." Henderson rested his case with a sober nod. He had tried to sound mature and reasonable throughout.

"You forget about the kids, Kevin," Duhl said.

"Oh yeah, they—"

"Both our boys recognized Her immediately," Duhl said, cutting off Henderson. "They had seen Her before but hadn't said anything because they were afraid we'd just laugh at them."

"Did they think it was Our Lady, too?"

"Uh, yeah."

"They sure did," Henderson said emphatically.

"Well, what happened to you while you were sitting out there in your car? What did She do?" Father Lombardy kept asking questions, partly to gain time to sort out this new information in his mind, and partly in the hopes of finding a flaw, an inconsistency in their story. Something he could use to pry it loose and dismantle it. It was out of hand, all right, way out of hand. These people were trying to form a spiritual posse.

"Nothing," Henderson replied blankly, as if the question was peculiar. "Nothing at all. She was just there, that's all."

"We didn't move," Duhl said. "At first we didn't know what to think, so we didn't get out of the car."

"But you didn't back up and drive away either."

"No," Henderson said. "I had it in reverse but I didn't move. First, it didn't move towards us and it didn't seem harmful Secondly, I would have probably banged into a tree or something if I tried to reverse on that dark back road at night." Henderson had his story well worked out.

"How long were you there—was She there?"

"Five, ten minutes. Hard to tell, but not long. Then She... vanished."

"That's right," Duhl said. "Faded away."

Father Lombardy noticed that Father Connors sat calmly and quietly through this whole discussion. He had heard all this before. Maybe, even, he wanted to believe in it. The other two men present, Schreiber and Mikenas, had also heard it all before as was obvious from their clumsily-contrived looks of interest and surprise at various points when either Duhl or Henderson were talking. At one moment Father Lombardy had noticed Mikenas looking at Duhl with an expression of mock-wonder on his face, brow furrowed very much like Stan Laurel's in uncertainty. Father Lombardy had turned away quickly and asked another question, to avoid bursting into laughter. Now that everyone had apparently finished talking for the time being, that comic image came back to the young priest's mind. It was like a drawing-room charade, utter nonsense.

"Well, I'm sure you saw it," Father Lombardy began. "However, I'm not at all convinced that you saw Our Lady. Something, yes, but not Our Lady." Duhl and Henderson were shaking their heads in disagreement.

"Before you go too far, Father Lombardy, there is more you should know." Father Connors had at last spoken.

"What's that?"

"Several of the children have reported that the apparition speaks."

"I heard about that. Joey Pomar says he heard voices but he couldn't understand them. I doubt very much that he heard anything. As I said, and as I'm sure these men know, it is an unusual and impressive sight, whatever it is, and it can easily set the imagination racing."

"My kid understood it," Schreiber said suddenly, aggressively. "And so did lots of other kids."

"What?"

"Apparently," Father Connors said, as calm and smooth as ever, "several of the children have heard this presence speak to them."

"Really? What did it have to say to them?" Father Lombardy tried to make it sound as sarcastic as possible.

"That she is Our Lady, the Virgin Mary and Mother of God," Schreiber replied. "No doubt about it," he added for good measure.

"That's too much," Father Lombardy said flatly. "I can't believe that."

"I don't think it'll do much good for us to sit around arguing with each other any further," Father Connors said. "Father Lombardy, a number of parents and children are going to Mason's Mill on Saturday morning, as they believe that Our Lady will appear there. Do you know the place?"

"I do. It's an old abandoned mill that hasn't been used for about a hundred years and there isn't much left of it, aside from the foundation and, of course, the stream. Local farmers stripped the wood long ago, or most of it anyhow."

"I want you to go there, too."

"I'll be there, Father, I'll be glad to go. This matter has to be sorted out, the sooner the better. And I'm sure we'll find it isn't Our Lady."

After everyone had left but the two priests, Father Connors said: "You're very upset."

"Of course I am. I think this whole business is crazy and dangerous. There was a minor scandal in Garabandal, and we don't want anything like that here."

"No, of course not. But you're also upset because it has all gotten out of your hands a bit, isn't that right, Father?" Lombardy's face reddened, but the pastor continued quickly, so that the young priest wouldn't have time to deny it, "I will not be there with you on Saturday."

"If this situation is to be handled properly," Father Lombardy said, "it's no good just sending me out there. Higher authority should be brought in, the sooner the better."

"As a matter of fact, William, I have been on to the Chancery twice. These things do have to be reported immediately. I spoke to them after you came to me the first time and again this afternoon, after Mr. Henderson phoned me."

"What did the Chancery say?"

"They will have their own observer at Mason's Mill on Saturday."

"Am I the local guide?"

"No, you probably won't even see him. They're a fairly independent crowd at the Chancery, I'm afraid."

"Yes," Father Lombardy said.

CHAPTER EIGHT

"When does the show start?" Dave Lutz asked. His eyes were still puffy with sleep but he felt alert and wide awake. A punch jug balanced on his knees, which in turn were wedged against the dashboard of his tiny car.

"I don't know exactly," Martin Lasker said, sitting on a large flat stone alongside Lutz's open car door. He looked at his watch. It was quarter to nine in the morning and they had been there since eight. "Nobody seems to know."

"An anonymous tip, eh?" Lutz turned the valve on the jug and poured himself a Bloody Mary—his third.

"Well, no. Plenty of people are saying it will take place this morning—this appearance. But nobody seems to know who found out first, who heard the word."

"What am I doing out here?" Lutz said. "She won't appear. I mean, I saw them, so I don't disbelieve in the thing. But they didn't look like the Virgin Mary to me."

"Maybe you saw the Trinity." Lasker smiled. "Maybe the whole gang is going to come down from on high."

"Screw that, you don't believe it either."

"No, I don't," Lasker admitted. "But it is the most interesting explanation we've had so far."

"I still like flying saucers better, although they didn't look like that either. What am I doing here? It's Saturday morning, damn it. I should be sleeping."

"And miss a genuine miracle?"

"Miracle my eye. If it was a miracle they'd stage it on primetime television, not in the middle of the night." Lutz shifted the jug to the car floor and scrunched down lower in his seat, eyes closed.

"Quite a few people out there already," Martin Lasker said. He looked across the uneven field to Mason's Mill, a ruin of mossy stones and rotted timbers. Only the stream kept going strongly. Lasker could hear as well as see it splashing down where the mill-wheel once was.

"Are they parking their cars behind me?" Lutz looked around. They were on a rutted dirt passageway nearly a mile from the main road. "Damn it, we'll be the last ones out of here." There were thirty or forty people standing around the Mill and quite a few cars lined up down the dirt road.

"Well, it's a nice place for a picnic," Martin Lasker said, not really believing it.

"Isn't there some way we can keep people out of there? It is private property, after all." Ned Hanley dropped his cigarette butt in the plastic coffee-cup and listened for the tiny hiss.

"Yeah, but the Masons don't have it posted for no trespassing, and it's all wild country, not cultivated, and the Masons are in Florida or somewhere. Besides, that road is a public right-of-way."

"Yeah, but it's still private property, and part of our job is to protect private property. Isn't that so?"

"Ned, I'd like to do it. I even talked to the Mayor about it," Sturdevent said, stretching the fact considerably.

"You did?"

"There's no way we can go up there and turn people out as if were guarding Buckingham Palace. That'd only cause more trouble. All we can do is go along, try to persuade people to go home and when they don't, at least make sure they don't start cutting it up and making a mess."

It had been a rough week for Sturdevent, and today promised to be the worst day yet. He had been under steady pressure to come up with something in the Richter case, but it remained as unbreakable as the Donner death. He and Hanley had been at each other's throats all week and the only reason they were comparatively civil this morning was because they were both so tired.

What was worse, Sturdevent knew his home life was deteriorating rapidly. He snapped at the kids, when he bothered to say anything at all. His wife kept her distance, which was considerate but cool.

This damn religious thing had blown up virtually overnight. Thank God his own kids were not involved. Protestant kids didn't get up to that kind of nonsense. Now everybody in town thinks they've seen something, whether it's the Mother of God or an expedition from Venus. And Millville, his town, was cropping up in news reports around the state. "A town of murder and miracles," one television commentator had said the other night, greatly upsetting Sturdevent— and the Mayor, who had telephoned the Chief immediately and bitched for twenty minutes.

Sturdevent looked at his desk diary. He was due to take a week's vacation, starting next Monday, but that was postponed now. He'd take both weeks together in August. With any luck.

Hanley, who had been watching his cigarette butt float around in an inch of cold coffee, suddenly said: "Oh, I forgot to tell you. I finally got that priest, Father Lombardy, on the telephone last night."

"Yeah? And?"

"He thinks the whole thing is crazy, but he says he did see the thing."

"Him too." Sturdevent was careful not to make a crack about Catholics; Hanley was one and they had squabbled too much already. "It appears you and I are the only ones who haven't seen it yet."

"That's right."

"What does he think it is?"

"Pollution. Some kind of gas cloud of poisonous chemicals. He'll be there today."

Sturdevent grunted. Pollution. It made neither more nor less sense than anything else he had heard or thought of since this trouble started. The one thing it now seemed certain not to be was a nice, old-fashioned murderer, walking around with a blood-stained dagger in his hand. Too bad.

Hanley ran one thumb along the line of his jaw, feeling for small patches of stubble he might have missed shaving this morning. Sturdevent looked like he wanted to sit here in the office all morning. Why weren't they on their way already? Still, Hanley needn't worry. It was Sturdevent's problem. If they arrived too late—for what?—it would be Sturdevent's fault. Hanley wasn't going to say anything to the Chief.

How the hell did I miss that, he thought, rubbing a spot of growth just under his chin.

———

"Idobannahabagonerrayatome," he said.

"*Stuart.*" Marge Calder stood, half-dressed. "Are you getting up or not?" He didn't move. Marge resumed dressing. "You're going to miss it, and you'll be sorry afterwards that you didn't come."

"Mmmnaffalugmmmn."

"Well, I'm not missing it. I'll take the car. Stuart, do you hear me? I may be out all morning." He was sleeping soundly, his face buried in the pillow. How can he breathe, she thought, turning his head sideways. What a nuisance. She didn't want to go alone, but at the same time she was determined not to miss it. She knew that plenty of people had now seen what she saw, and it excited her. For one thing, it couldn't be the Virgin Mary, as some people were saying. That was just too silly for words. But if people could think that, then it must be as remarkable and special as she had thought when she saw it. Now, if all went well, she would finally see it close up. Maybe it wasn't a flying saucer and maybe it was, but it was bound to be something really new and strange, whatever it was.

It was nice of Martin Lasker to call her up and tell her about it. She had only glanced at the piece in the newspaper—she didn't read about religion, after all, and that's what the article had looked like it was about.

"Good-bye," she called to her husband. He didn't move. Sometimes he's so prosaic, Marge Calder thought, closing the front door of the house behind her. When she told him about the reporter taking down her story about the lights, he just chuckled at that. Stu was a happy, easy-going guy. So happy and easy-going it might just become a problem. Was he going to be increasingly dull for the rest of their lives? Marge Calder hoped not.

"Mind if I join you?" Father Slomcenski asked, emerging from the dining room after Father Lombardy. "I know Father Connors asked you specifically to go to the thing today, but I'd like to tag along and see what happens for myself. Makes a change."

"Sure," Father Lombardy replied, without enthusiasm. "Let's go."

"Great. I cancelled my golf game. This thing really sounds weird, doesn't it? I gather you don't think much of it?"

"Of course not," Father Lombardy answered, perhaps a little too harshly. "A bunch of runaway imaginations. The thing was bad enough when just the children were involved, but now that adults are trying to get into the act it's almost criminal." His own words surprised him. Father Slomcenski nodded agreeably but said nothing. "Don't you think so?"

"I guess so. The whole thing seems too fantastic for a nice quiet middle-class town."

Father Lombardy switched on the FM radio in his car as they pulled out of the rectory parking lot, and found a station broadcasting pleasant orchestral music. Mendelssohn, perhaps, he thought. He turned the volume up slightly, to discourage talk.

He wasn't happy to have Father Slomcenski with him, especially at such short notice. The other priest was a nice fellow and they got along well, but his appearance this Saturday morning aroused suspicion and uneasiness in Father Lombardy. Was Father Connors behind it? A quiet word to Father Slomcenski? Did the pastor doubt Father Lombardy that much? Was he that devious? Father Lombardy doubted it. After all, Father Connors could have come along himself if he had wanted to—he wasn't frail by any means.

Perhaps Father Slomcenski's presence was as innocent as he made it seem. And he could be very helpful, when it came to that. He was young, strong, burly, a former high-school football star. If things got out of hand at Mason's Mill, Father Slomcenski would be a good man to have around. In spite of the fact that Father Lombardy had all but convinced himself with his own argument that the strange phenomenon was nothing more than a cloud of chemical gas, he still did worry that it might be something else, something much less explicable and infinitely more dangerous. Something *could* happen, and if it did, many people would be looking to him, as the representative of the Church, to handle it, to explain and resolve it. In that case he would be very grateful for Father Slomcenski's presence on the scene. The theological irony of the situation didn't escape him.

But another question came to mind. Wouldn't their presence at the Mill lend a certain credibility to the budding Marianist following? For that matter, was it already a movement, a cult? Newspapers might well report that they were there, and so imply that the whole thing had the tacit approval of the parish priests. That was something Father Connors would have considered—or should have.

"You look pretty worried, Bill. Cheer up," Father Slomcenski broke the silence. He smiled, but the net effect was only to enhance Father Lombardy's suspicion.

On Eight Mile Road they ran into traffic.

By nine-thirty the crowd had passed the one hundred mark, Martin Lasker estimated. Already a lot more than he had expected. Most of these people were probably just curious, but as the young reporter walked through the crowd he could feel tension in the air. Even the curious thought something would happen.

Near the Mill he saw a group of children seated on the grass. They were dressed in white, a fairly even collection of boys and girls, numbering about thirty. A ring of adults, probably parents stood around the group of children. These were the serious core of people around whom today's miracle or fiasco or non-event would evolve. They were dressed for church-going, and they didn't mingle with the other people who strolled around in sports-shirts and Bermuda shorts, some carrying cameras.

A man named Henderson had phoned in the news about today's gathering to the newspaper. Martin Lasker asked one man if he knew Henderson. No. Nor did a second, but the reporter was lucky on the third try. An elderly woman beamed and pointed out Henderson, a squat, middle-aged individual with a crewcut that would probably check out as perfectly flat with a carpenter's level.

"Mr. Henderson?"

"Yeah?" The large man turned to face Martin Lasker.

"I'm from the *Millville News*."

"Yeah."

"I'd like to ask you a few questions." Martin switched on his recorder and held his microphone halfway between Henderson and himself.

"Yeah, uh, okay, what do you want to know?" Henderson looked mildly uncomfortable but at the same time he felt he should cooperate. After all, he had notified the newspaper.

"What's going to happen here today?"

"We believe that the Virgin Mary, the Mother of God, will appear on this site this morning." A well-practiced line by now.

"What makes you think that?"

"The children know. She has already appeared to many of them and She told them to bring us here today."

"What if She doesn't come?"

"Doesn't matter. She will appear, if not today then another day, soon. But She will appear today."

"You seem very sure of that."

"I am. It's a modern miracle."

"Why should She appear here, or anywhere?"

"She obviously has a message for mankind and has chosen this place. I don't know why, but She has… has chosen this place to appear and after today this land will be sacred ground for all time." Henderson said it with an air of finality, as if there were no other possible conclusion.

"Do you know what Her message will be?" Lasker mentally congratulated himself for getting the question out without cutting a smile.

"No, of course not, but I'm sure it will be of importance for all mankind." Henderson kept looking over Lasker's shoulder, as if looking for someone in the crowd. The reporter ignored it and kept the questions coming.

"But wasn't Mary supposed to have given a message at Fatima? A message that has never been revealed by Rome in the years since?"

"Uh, well, I think that's right, yeah, but I'm not really in a position to comment on that. I believe we will be given a message today. That's all I can say about that"

"Are you aware that some people think flying saucers have been visiting Millville, not the Mother of God?"

"That's ridiculous," Henderson asserted. "We knew that some curiosity-seekers and cranks would turn out here today but that's okay. In fact, we hoped they would. They'll see and they'll learn, and there'll be no doubt about it. But I don't think you'll see any flying saucers or little green men."

"Have you or any of your friends been in touch with the Church about this—either in the parish or with the archbishop's office in Hartford?"

"Of course. We've spoken with Father Connors, the pastor of St Jude's."

"And what does he say?"

"Well, you have to realize that they can't come out and say anything, not at first. They have to be cautious in a sensitive matter like this, and they have to talk to their superiors and there's a whole big political thing there, you know. But that's understandable, that's why the Church is what it is. They proceed at their own holy pace."

"Does that mean Father Connors discouraged you or doesn't approve?"

"No, not at all. It isn't a matter of approving or not approving at this stage."

"What do you think he thinks?"

"You'll have to ask him that." Henderson looked pleased with himself. He had once heard a politician say that on television and it had seemed to work well.

"I know you think there'll be a message today."

"That's right."

"But are you also expecting some sort of sign or miracle?"

"I don't know. Maybe and maybe not. I really can't presume to think what the Virgin Mary might have in mind. I don't see any wheel-chairs or people on crutches here, though." It wouldn't do to be too grand in one's predictions, Henderson thought. They'll just say we're a bunch of wild-eyed holy-rollers.

"Did your children see Her?"

"Yes, they did."

"Did She say anything to them?"

"Him, my son. No, She didn't."

"Does that strike you as odd?"

"No. I wouldn't expect Our Lady to be a gabber. She has a message for mankind and She'll deliver it."

"Thank you." Lasker got Henderson's full name, address and telephone number. "I may come back to you for more comments."

"Sure," Henderson said.

Marge Calder had to walk a considerable distance to reach the site at Mason's Mill. Vehicles were lined up all the way down the dirt road that ran through Mason property and she could see that there would be a terrible snarl-up when everyone tried to go home. Walking in from the main road would be wiser, she had thought, but she hadn't realized how far it was, and now she was hot and sweaty. Maybe this wasn't such a good idea after all.

There must be a couple of hundred people present, she thought, as she looked around. Plenty of familiar faces, seen around town before, but no one she knew to talk to. Then she spotted Martin Lasker standing by a car at the edge of the field. She walked over to him.

"Hello," she said. "Remember me?"

"Hi. Sure I do."

"Thanks for telling me about this."

"No trouble."

"I'm anxious to see—well, if anything happens."

"So am I, and a lot of other people."

"What a crowd," she agreed.

Dave Lutz, who had by now finished the jug of Bloody Marys, studied this woman from his seat in the car. When she looked at him absently, he smiled. "I'm Dave Lutz." She nodded politely.

"Oh, sorry," Martin Lasker said. "Dave Lutz, a friend of mine. This is Mrs. Calder."

"Marge. Hi."

"Hi. You think—" but he realized that if he mentioned flying saucers he'd probably embarrass both Lasker and the woman. "What do you think it is, or will happen, or both?"

"I really don't know," Marge answered, thinking that Lutz had very watery eyes.

"But you've seen it. Yes?" He knew he wasn't making a great impression on Marge Calder. Pity, she was good looking. And out of high school.

"Yes, I've seen the lights, the blue whatever it is," she replied. "But from far away, miles really and I don't have the slightest idea what they are." She turned to Martin Lasker but he was busy scanning the crowd.

"Kind of like a picnic, or a Flag Day outing, isn't it?" Lutz said, to make conversation.

"Yes, it almost looks like that," she answered.

The sound of voices rising in unison began to spread through the air, making itself heard above the buzz of conversation. The children by the Mill were singing hymns.

"Listen," Marge Calder said.

"Don't tell me they have to summon Her to appear," Lutz cracked. "Or maybe this is just the warm-up band." Marge Calder didn't smile. Oh well, Lutz sighed.

"There's the police," Lasker said. Marge followed the line of his gaze and Lutz craned his neck out of the open car-door to see. "The two guys in front are Sturdevent, the police chief, and Hanley, the captain," Lasker explained.

"Looks like they have the entire police force of Millville with them," Marge said, shading her eyes with her hand.

"Four... eight," Lasker counted. "I think there's about twenty altogether on the force. Eight is a lot, especially on week-end rates."

"Are they going to try and break it up?" Marge Calder wondered aloud.

It was worse than Sturdevent had expected in even his gloomiest of moods, and he knew it before he and Hanley reached the Mill Road cut-off. Dave Corwin had come on the police radio saying there was a jam of cars trying to get in, and that some were even driving into the fields. Sturdevent had immediately given the order to refuse all access and start sending people home. Dirty work for Corwin again, but that's the way it would have to be. Sturdevent then radioed in to the station to call out additional policemen.

"Sounds like they're going to make a carnival out of it," Ned Hanley said.

"Oh no, they won't," Sturdevent rasped back. "Not in Millville, they won't."

When the other policemen arrived at the cut-off Chief Sturdevent led them on the last bumpy stretch of the journey to Mason's Mill.

"Well, well, well," Hanley said, sounding almost happy to see so many people at the site.

"We've got to break this up," Sturdevent said. This was too much. There would be trouble with the Mayor and the newspapers, regardless of which way he chose to handle the situation. A small gathering of religious fanatics had grown in no time to a major assembly. There were several hundred people present.

It annoyed Sturdevent that he was again coming around to Hanley's viewpoint. These people should have been prevented from coming in the first place; now they would have to go, and it would be just too bad if a few sensibilities were ruffled in the process. He had been maneuvered into another corner.

"You can't break this up," Hanley said calmly. "Not now, you can't"

"What? What are you talking about?" Sturdevent couldn't believe his ears.

The other patrolmen stood around anxiously, hands on hips, waiting for someone to give them definite orders.

"You can't break this up," Hanley repeated. "There's too many people here now. You'd have to call in the National Guard, or at least have another couple of dozen men. There aren't enough of us to move this crowd. Besides, we don't have any kind of proper crowd-control equipment."

"Damn it all," Sturdevent said. Naturally Hanley would change his own mind in turn, just to make life more difficult for the Chief. "Fan out and tell these people to get out of here," Sturdevent told the policemen. "Tell them this is private property and they are trespassing, and they have to go home."

"You can't arrest them all," Hanley said.

The men lingered, still uncertain. They knew it was an impossible job. People would just wander around, looking as if they were heeding the police instructions, but no one would actually go. And the situation was hardly right for arresting people.

Sturdevent, too, realized that police action at this stage would be largely ineffectual but he had decided that something had to be done. If he was going to be roasted later it wouldn't be for total inaction. He could say he did try to get the people out but that he hadn't enough men to do the job.

"I know we can't arrest them all I don't want anyone arrested unless they give you active trouble. But I want you to get out there and move them. I don't care if you have to take them out one at a time and lead them to their cars, I want them out of here. So get going."

"Why don't you use the bull-horn?" Hanley asked. "We have got that, in the car."

"I will in a minute, if it's necessary." Sturdevent wouldn't use the bull-horn, that was for sure. He didn't intend to make matters worse by sounding silly in public.

"Chief Sturdevent?" It was Martin Lasker.

"What?"

"Are you going to break this up?"

"Nice job your paper did, boy, getting everybody and his big brother-in-law out here this morning."

Lasker ignored the crack. After his last run-in with Chief Sturdevent he had decided it was silly and unprofessional to worry about the hurt feelings of public servants, especially someone like this man, who was supposed to be in charge. "Are you going to break it up?" he repeated the question forcefully.

"We'll see." To Hanley he said, "Let's get going, Ned." Then Sturdevent had a bright idea, and it cheered him immensely. "Wait a minute. Ned, you get the bull-horn hooked up and tell these folks to scram." He should have thought of this the second Hanley brought it up.

"Me?" Hanley was taken aback.

"Yeah, you." That would fix Hanley. "I'm going to try and find the people who are running this show. If we can get them out of here, the others may lose interest and leave."

Hanley looked disgusted, but he began walking back to the police car. Sturdevent set off for the Mill with Lasker by his side.

This kid tags along everywhere, like a goddamn cocker spaniel, Sturdevent thought. "I hope you realize how stupid this whole thing is making Millville look," he growled.

"Something is going on in this town, Chief. A lot of people have already seen things, including a friend of mine."

"Friend?" Sturdevent made the word sound impossible. "Things? What things?"

"You know, the—"

"The Virgin Mary, I suppose."

Lasker decided that anything he said would only further aggravate Sturdevent's foul mood. They continued to work their way through the crowd, but before they reached the Mill they stopped. Everyone stood still. The singing ended.

In the air over the Mill a small but expanding globe of blue light formed. Within seconds it seemed as large as a house, floating in the air. The crowd gasped in unison. There it was.

The people closest to the object, the children and their parents, fell to the ground and began to pray aloud. Others in the crowd followed suit, but most people remained standing, staring transfixed.

So that's it, Sturdevent thought. It does exist. He knew immediately it was real, not a trick. No-one could rig that. The light burned so brilliantly he felt as if he was standing in a dark room, but he knew he was out in a field on a sunny day. It was real all right, whatever it was. Two conflicting emotions welled up in him. First, a sense of relief that at long last he could see it and know it was real. No policeman could be held responsible for that thing. It had terrorised his town and he hadn't caught it, but now he could see why. And so could everyone else. He was just as helpless and he felt as if a great burden had been removed from his shoulders. At the same time, fear grew within him. This was out of his hands now, he knew that, but who could deal with it? Who would protect them? Who would—save them? As the blue light hovered over the Mill, Sturdevent thought of his wife and children. They were at home, but no longer safe. Nobody was safe. He realized he was shaking badly.

Martin Lasker knew he should be describing everything into his tape recorder but he couldn't move. His eyes were held to the incredible sight. It was beautiful, and there were shapes, or at least movements, within the thing, as if it were alive. He could understand now why some people thought it was the Virgin Mary or some such godly being. It looked like it *should* be. It was—perfect was the word that came to mind. A perfect, beautiful entity.

Marge Calder, who had still been standing near Lutz's car when the blue light appeared, now began to work her way through the crowd to get a closer look. It was much more impressive than she had imagined.

"Better stay back," Dave Lutz called after her, but she ignored him. "Damn it all." He slammed his car door shut and went after her.

Father Lombardy and Father Slomcenski had just made their way by foot up the dirt road and now stood at the edge of the field.

"It is... I'll be..." Father Slomcenski murmured quietly.

"Bigger than before," Father Lombardy said grimly. He began to move towards the Mill, but it was difficult going. There were so many people, and they all were moving slowly towards the blue light. Now the cloud seemed to be in the air everywhere, sinking lower like a fog. But it continued to bum brightly only at the point of origin, over Mason's Mill. Father Lombardy felt close to panic. The air of menace was terrifying, but he seemed to be the only person sensing it. What could he do? It was too late; perhaps too late for all of them.

"Oh God," he said aloud when, a few seconds later, he saw the first body flop through the air like a thrown toy.

The spell was broken and people began running and shouting. By the Mill, the wind spread in a widening gyre, casting people aside casually, churning up clumps of sod and stones. Chief Sturdevent, who had not quite reached the Mill, was close enough to notice that even water from the stream was splashed and sprayed about. Everything within the area of the blue light was hit, and the area of the circle was increasing.

It didn't take the crowd long to scatter, either several hundred yards away into the fields or behind the line of cars on the dirt road. There they stood and gaped, like Ned Hanley who had not moved from the large boulder he had climbed onto. The bull-horn hung idly in his hand.

The blue light stopped growing, but it remained at the site for nearly twenty minutes, burning like some grotesquely enormous flare. By the time it faded swiftly away most people had fled, although a number still stood watching from a safe distance.

In the trampled grass and dug-up dirt around the Mill were many more bodies.

CHAPTER NINE

Sturdevent hobbled into the lobby of the police station. He wore casts on his left ankle, which had suffered a slight fracture, and on his left hand, the wrist of which had been broken cleanly. He glanced up at the wall clock and saw that it was a few minutes before noon. Just over twenty-four hours after the incident at Mason's Mill.

The room was crammed with people, mostly newsmen. There were others, though, he knew that—politicians, irate citizens and God only knew who else. They had been camping there for hours. Sturdevent didn't like the idea of facing them, but he knew he had to—they would wait until he appeared, and to delay too long would only make matters worse.

He carried two sheets of paper in his good hand. One was an information sheet Hanley had prepared for him and the other was a statement he had written himself. As he stepped gingerly to the makeshift podium, the crowd seemed to lean forward towards him. Cameras popped and clicked, and he tried to ignore it all. *Pretend you're addressing an empty room. But be careful.* Several people in front started calling him by name and asking questions.

"Just a minute," Sturdevent said, holding up his two sheets of paper. "Can I have quiet, please, for a minute?"

Everyone was suddenly silent, so quickly and so completely that Sturdevent was almost startled. He was aware of the sweat trickling down his sides. The heat and tension in the room was painful to him. All those faces looking at him, ready to draw on him, drain him, pick him apart piece by piece until there was nothing left. He felt as if he might vomit.

"Before I fill you in on the information we have as it stands at the moment, I'd like to make a statement. Then you can ask questions, and we'll answer them as best we can." Everyone remained still. Sturdevent held up the sheet of paper which contained his own handwriting and began to read in a loud, overly formal voice.

"What happened in this town during the last couple of weeks leading up to and including yesterday is a tragedy of major proportions. A deadly force is loose and it poses a threat to each and every one of us. But this is not a criminal case. No one person or conspiracy of persons is behind this force. No one could have known, until this force came out into the open yesterday morning, what we were up against. Over the last two weeks this police force made every reasonable effort to solve the mystery of the violent deaths of three people in Millville, and we weren't able to do it. Yesterday we found out why. Whatever it is, and I have to tell you that we do not know yet what it is, we will face it and overcome it We have asked for, and we expect to receive, the help of state and federal authorities.

"This office has been flooded with calls suggesting that yesterday's incident was the result of witchcraft, and I saw on some of last night's news reports that some people think there's something strange and evil about the town of Millville, that's causing this terrible business. I want to state categorically that I do not believe this is true. There is no witchcraft here and there is nothing unusual about Millville. This town is as normal, as ordinary and as sane as any other town in the country. What has been happening here is outside of us, a force of nature gone berserk, perhaps. But no Salem witchcraft, no evil, twisted minds, no Charles Mansons or anything else like that. Millville is clean, not foul. Millville is healthy, not sick. Millville may be in trouble, but it is not a monster or a freak.

"I would ask those of you who have come from out of town, especially those of you working with newspapers, radio or television, to help us through our ordeal. I'm sure you will."

Sturdevent turned to his fact sheet. That didn't go so bad, he thought. At least they listened, and he had heard only a little fidgeting from the audience. It should even impress the Mayor, a statement like that. More than the kind of thing a cop like Hanley could ever come up with.

"Chief, how many people died yesterday?"

"Thirteen so far. Thirty-two other people are in the hospital with injuries. Four are critical, I believe, but I think some of the others may already have been sent home."

"Do you believe that this thing is in any way supernatural?"

"No."

"Why was the gathering at Mason's Mill allowed to take place in the first place?"

Bastard. That had to come. Sturdevent had worked out a pat answer he knew wouldn't satisfy anyone for long. "We were under the impression that it was to be a small religious event, nothing like what developed."

"Is it true you have an All-Points Bulletin out on the Virgin Mary?"

There were a few muffled laughs from the crowd. Sturdevent couldn't see who had asked the question. He decided the best thing to do was to ignore it.

"Anything else?" he asked levelly.

"Are you going to release the names of the dead people?"

"In a couple of hours, I expect. We haven't been able to contact the next of kin in each case yet, but I think we will within another couple of hours."

"How many were children?"

"Eight."

"Is it true that one of the persons who was killed was a priest?"

"Yes."

"If you don't think the thing is supernatural, and it's not purely criminal, then what is it?"

"As I said, we don't know what it is."

"What's your personal opinion?"

"I don't know. I'm a policeman, not a scientist."

"It's been said that you looked into the possibility that the Russians were involved in one of the murders. Is it your feeling that they — Russian scientists — could be behind this whole matter?"

"We have no evidence at this time to link the Russians or any other foreign power to the events in this town."

"Then are you specifically ruling that possibility out?"

"I'm not ruling out anything."

Lasker and Lutz wandered out of the police station and sat down on the front steps of the building. They had heard enough of Sturdevent's press conference and had decided to get some fresh air.

"Have you noticed all the out-of-state license plates in town now?" Lutz asked.

"Yeah."

"We're really on the map now."

"I'm afraid so."

"How'd you like his speech?"

"Ridiculous."

"Bad composition, I thought. I'd give him a D for it if he handed it in for grading."

"Trying to sound like Churchill, but it didn't come off." Lasker fiddled with the dials on his portable cassette recorder. He had used the second side to record Sturdevent's statement—the first side was full already. He must have left it on during yesterday's trouble at the Mill.

A tall, gangling youth slouched along the sidewalk, spotted the two men and stopped.

"Hiya, Mr. Lutz," he said.

"Nardello," Lutz said with distaste. The student wore a tee-shirt that carried the message: *I choked Linda Lovelace.*

"I saw ya there yesterday, Mr. Lutz."

"Did you?"

"Yeah. How do you explain it? That thing, I mean? Think it's from outer space?" Nardello tried to look intelligent and concerned, but failed to carry it off.

"I don't know." This thing must really be getting to me, Lutz thought, if I can't even put down Nardello.

"I thought it was a mass hallucination," Nardello said firmly. "You know, hysteria. Everybody expected to see something, so they did, and then some of them got trampled when the crowd panicked."

"Did you tell the police?" Lutz asked indifferently.

"Hell, no, they'd only laugh at me. They were there too, you know."

"Didn't you see the blue light too?" Martin Lasker queried.

"Sure, but I still think it wasn't real. Just a big... like a group trip, you know? It woulda been neat if some people didn't get hurt and stuff."

"That's your considered opinion, is it, Nardello?" Lutz was annoyed that the student, this one in particular, was making more sense than he felt capable of at the present time.

"Yeah. I guess so," Nardello said. For several minutes no one spoke and the student got tired of standing around. "I'll see ya, Mr. Lutz. I gotta go."

"Good-bye." Lutz pronounced the syllables as two separate words.

"That's an interesting argument," Lasker said, after Nardello had shuffled out of sight.

Lutz snorted. "You don't believe that."

"Makes as much sense—or nonsense—as anything else I've heard or thought of yet"

"That thing was real to me—in the classroom, in the field with Sandra and at the Mill yesterday. Ask your friend Marge, she's in the hospital. Ask that guy who got killed and the married couple over at Heritage House. Ask them all if it was a hallucination."

"I'm not saying it is," Lasker replied defensively. Dave had been very touchy since yesterday. "I just think it might as well be considered as a possibility, along with everything else. Hallucinations can be very real If something could make them even more real, sort of super-real, crossing from the mental to the physical world—ah…" Lasker waved his hand dismissively. The argument seemed to fall apart like sand. Like everything else connected with the Millville Monster, as one radio announcer had termed it, there was too much improbability. And yet, the most improbable thing of all, the Monster had so far killed sixteen people.

"Hello, Lasker."

It was Ned Hanley, with a cup of orange crush in one hand, a cigarette in the other and a smile on his face.

"Captain Hanley," Lasker acknowledged.

"Who's this?" Hanley sat down on the step, gesturing with his cigarette to Lutz. "Jimmy Olson?"

"Dave Lutz," Lasker replied. "Teaches at the high school."

"Oh, hi," Hanley smiled. "I thought everybody around here now was a newspaperman or a cop, and I can tell you aren't a cop." Lutz scowled and resumed staring at the sidewalk. "Too hot in there,"

Hanley continued to Lasker. "They're really giving the Chief a hard time."

Before Lasker could think of anything to say, a short, elderly man came up to him, grabbed his arm urgently and said, "Are you a reporter?"

"Uh, yes, I am."

"You must listen to me. I can tell you what it is."

Hanley and Lutz watched with skepticism evident on their faces. "Who are you?" Lasker asked.

"Doctor Gabriel Acevedo, and I have made a study of these things. You must hear what I have to say."

"All right," Lasker said reluctantly. "What do you think it is?"

"Jinn," Dr. Acevedo said simply, and his eyes lit up with the word.

"Gin?" Lutz chuckled.

"J-i-n-n," Dr. Acevedo spelled it out. "Jinn. In Arabian mythology the universe is full of jinns, which are for all practical purposes demons. They may be friendly or hostile, and I believe what we have here are malevolent jinns terrorising your town of Millville." Dr. Acevedo paused to catch his breath and then continued. "The commonly held and ignorant view today is to think of genies in a bottle or a lamp, and so on. You know that, everyone does. But the real jinn can assume any different form it wishes, and it takes great pleasure in harming mankind."

"Listen, Gob-reel," Ned Hanley interjected. "I'm a policeman and you can't expect me to swallow this crap."

"A policeman! Good. I'm telling you it's true. The jinns are demons born of fire, they can become visible or invisible at will and they have a vast range of supernatural powers. What happened yesterday was a display of just that. A malignant jinn."

"So the Arabs are doing it to us," Lutz said. "It figures."

"Believe me," Dr. Acevedo urged. "I think this town is in the possession of two, three, maybe more jinns. They have, as it were, marked this place as their own, and that means your whole town is in great danger. Great, great danger."

Hanley sneered and lit another cigarette. The town was in danger all right, from cranks and oddballs like this guy. Bullshit was the order of the day, he reflected.

"I'm telling you," Dr. Acevedo repeated.

Martin Lasker had observed all this without saying anything. There was certainly something peculiar about Dr. Acevedo, but he didn't have the fanatic gleam of just another crank. Rather, he had the rumpled, pedantic air of an academic.

"Do you teach somewhere, Doctor?" Lasker inquired.

"Yes, Boston," the elderly man said quickly. "But I am not important. What is important is the jinn, and what they will do to you."

"What will they do to us, Doctor?" Lutz asked in a bored tone of voice.

"More damage, more trouble, and quite possibly more injuries or death to people."

"What should—assuming you're right—what should we do about the jinn?" Lasker found the idea intriguing. Perhaps there was a short news item in it—visiting professor warns of mythological demons, etc.

"Evacuate the town," Dr. Acevedo answered promptly. "That is the only safe, sure thing to do. You cannot try to fight them and you cannot hope to outlast them. Of course, they are prankish and impulsive, and they may leave of their own accord. But it wouldn't be safe to count on that."

"Well," Dave Lutz yawned. "We've had the Catholics and now the Moslems. Who's next—the Shintoists or the Christian Scientists?"

The pleasant drone of crickets drifted up on the evening breeze to Father Lombardy's room. He smoked cigarettes, one lit from the burnt-down end of the last. Harsh, untipped French cigarettes. He thought he was burning his throat away, steadily, systematically, and he didn't know why. It was something to do.

Father Slomcenski didn't deserve to die. Not then, not so pointlessly. He belonged in the land of the living, on the golf course where he probably would have been on any other Saturday morning. Any normal Saturday morning. In the land of the living. With the rest of the survivors.

A freak death in a freak situation.

"Gosh," Father Slomcenski had said when the crowd turned around and overwhelmed them. Both priests had gone down to the ground, it was impossible to escape—or so it had seemed at the time. Yet Father Lombardy survived, with bruises and cuts, whereas someone had stepped on Father Slomcenski's head, breaking his neck. It was that simple.

Father Lombardy had slept only in short, fitful bursts in the thirty-six hours since the incident at the Mill. He had been short and sharp with Father Connors, and in a brief moment of cruelty the pastor reminded him that he had been in touch with the Chancery, which had sent its own observers to Mason's Mill that day. Father Lombardy, feeling more useless than ever, remained in his room. He remembered reading books by people who had been through German concentration camps during World War II and the enormous anguish they had suffered because they had survived while their families and friends had perished. Now he too wondered why he was still living when Father Slomcenski had died on the ground next to him. It was hard to accept, and they hadn't even been close friends. Just—colleagues.

A daze—he had walked away in a daze. He had seen the thing twice now, and had felt its power. A power loose among the survivors. What was it? The unknown, and that in itself said everything. Father Lombardy knew now what had never occurred to him before—that there is no place for the unknown with man. Everything had to be something, capable of being named, tagged and put in place, if not actually explained and understood. Not pure knowledge, not Faust's dream, but something much more banal. An ability to cope and assign that suggests knowledge. Man can live with mysteries, in fact to a certain extent he needs them—the Holy Trinity or the Immaculate Conception, these things he could not know or understand but he could accept. They would fit in his picture of the universe.

But not this thing that had come on them like an evil visitation. That was a mystery, and it could not remain so. No one could stand it. Mysteries do not appear out of the sky, kill people, and disappear, without some answer, some explanation. You cannot call it the unknown and then forget about it. It's a warp, no, more than that, a vacuum in the fabric of reality. No, that's still not it, Father Lombardy thought. It's a kind of anti-reality that wreaks havoc with the normal course of events.

He remembered reading a magazine article about snake venom, which is almost pure protein. Protein is essential to life, so why should snake venom be so deadly to life? Because it was too much for the body to handle, it jammed the system, destroying instead of aiding life. It didn't fit the pattern. Conflicting signals resulted in total paralysis, breakdown and death. The blue cloud was like that, the pure protein of death.

Father Lombardy explored the analogy for a few moments, then lit another cigarette.

It wasn't an escaped cloud of chemical pollution, that much was certain. He regretted that fact because, although he never quite believed his own argument, he knew it was a good one, better than many he had heard. But it was irrelevant now.

What was it?

It had to be knowable, he was sure of that. Only God in His infinite ways was unknowable, and Father Lombardy was sure that the blue cloud was not God, the Virgin Mary or any of the angels.

What would the observer priests report back to the Chancery? He would enjoy hearing what they had to say. How could anyone be an expert at this?

The Devil? Demonology, possession, Satanism, witchcraft—no, it was none of these. Not unless the entire history, literature and mythology on the subject was wrong. Father Lombardy found it hard to believe in the Devil anyhow. It was a subject the Church tended to play down somewhat these days, as being rather old-fashioned. Positive thinking said you should stress the good, the holy, the right way, not build up gruesome tales of demons and evil spirits. Of course Evil existed, but to personify it too much was not a wise thing to do. No, the Devil, if he existed in the traditional sense, worked to a purpose. With cunning and arrogance. But the blue cloud merely appeared and disappeared, killing people mindlessly, aimlessly. It was a thing, and it had to be knowable.

Why had he left the scene again? Why was he so numb and unobservant both times he had encountered it? The questions came back to Father Lombardy's mind, again and again. Was he afraid of seeing something, of knowing?

He would go back. Even though it was now getting dark the sky would probably be quite bright and he might see something, or *feel* something, that would give him a better idea. He slipped on his loafers, tucked his shirt in his pants, took cigarettes and matches, and left the rectory.

As he drove through Millville, Father Lombardy recalled the times he had gone back to the clearing near Emerson School. He had seen nothing there on each return visit. And all he had felt was a little foolish. But this time might be different. For one thing, the blue light had been much bigger and brighter at Mason's Hill than it had been when he saw it with Joey Pomar. Joey Pomar—not listed among the dead, lucky boy. What did the Pomars think now of their Virgin Mary?

Even if this time was no different, Father Lombardy felt he had to go. Too late again, perhaps, but necessary. This thing had brought to light weaknesses in himself he hadn't known about, and it disturbed him. He had to get to the bottom of it. He had been a self-confident person; now he realized that that was false, a veneer behind which hid considerable doubt and confusion. He had been complacent; now he was restless. He had been a smooth-talker; now he was incoherent with other people. He had been an extrovert, a take-charge fellow; now he was withdrawn and unassertive—as witness his performance with Henderson and the other men in the rectory last week. This thing had snarled him up. Personally.

It was a good, clear night and the moon would help him at the Mill. When Father Lombardy turned into the dirt road he wondered if he would find police posted at the site. That might be a problem. Yes—he braked quickly. Just inside the turn-off the dirt road was blocked. The police had set up three lines of barricades, running from side to side. Too much trouble to move, he thought. There didn't seem to be anyone posted there, which was a good sign. He could drive back to the main road, swing into the field and hope to re-join the dirt road further along, as some people had done yesterday. But he might easily drive into a ditch in the dark and get stuck. He got out and walked.

The journey by foot seemed shorter than it had with Father Slomcenski yesterday morning, but that was probably because there were no cars along the dirt road to impede the pace. It was a cool evening but the priest worked up a light sweat as he hurried along.

When he came within a hundred yards of the Mill field he stopped in shadows and looked carefully around. He could see no one and the only sounds he heard were of the stream and the crickets. There was nobody on duty here, he was sure of it. Father Lombardy stepped out into the bright meadow.

Even in the silvery half-light he could easily see the jagged tear in the ground where the blue cloud had dug up the earth. He squatted down and felt it with his hand. The dirt was cool and damp, as expected, and it told him nothing. The surrounding grass was not much help either, having been trampled so much by the crowd.

Closer to the Mill, Father Lombardy saw several wooden stakes driven into the ground, each with a strip of white cloth tied to the top. Presumably they marked the spots where the dead bodies had been. Did they form a pattern? He walked around, examining the cluster of small flags from different angles but concluded that they didn't.

He walked to the stream and sat on one of the large foundation stones that had supported the Mill. It felt smooth and glassy, almost as if it had been polished with care. Had the blue cloud done that too, or simply the passage of time? This, he reckoned, was the place where the thing had materialized yesterday, directly over these stones. The whole area seemed so peaceful and pleasant now. Only the white flags served to remind...

Father Lombardy looked into the trees in the distance. Were lights flickering there? Yes. All over the place. But they were yellowish-orange and the thrill died in him as he immediately realized they were fire-flies. Lovely and harmless. Wait a minute! Both times he had seen the blue cloud he had noticed, as had everyone who saw it, that the center of the thing was brilliant, burning. As if it were alive, or—fire. Hadn't he thought of it as a burning light? Yes, of course he had. But why hadn't it actually burned anything? The bodies of the dead were not charred, unless the police were hiding that fact and he could think of no reason why they should. He felt the grass around him and found nothing to suggest it had been burned. Like a fire, but not a fire. Could it be some kind of natural phosphorescence, like fire-flies or certain deep-sea creatures? It seemed entirely possible, and Father Lombardy was elated with this new turn of thought. However, it was difficult to see how he could use it. The thing couldn't be some actual creature that no one had ever heard of before—could it? Appearing and disappearing at will, looking largely like a cloud of gas with a fire at the center... no, it was highly unlikely.

Unless... unless it was some kind of bizarre mutation, a once-only monstrosity compounded of—what?—swamp life and man-made poisons? Why not? In that case his original notion about pollution would be pretty much right. People were still in the process of finding out what terrible things chemical pollutants could do to animals and human beings. It was certainly conceivable that something far worse than anyone had hitherto imagined possible could in fact have come about, a kind of latter-day Frankenstein's monster.

He took out his notebook and by the moon's brilliant light wrote down the words *cold fire*.

Now Father Lombardy felt he was making genuine progress. Why had he tried to keep that line of thought down before? The religious and supernatural side, conjured up by people like Pomar, had intruded, distracting him. Throwback superstitions.

What was happening in Millville was an acutely social problem, he knew that now. He felt as if his mind had suddenly been cleared of cobwebs and dust. Weren't most of the problems a modern priest faced of a social nature? Birth control, abortion, drug abuse, ghetto crime—these things were manmade problems and issues, not religious. Of course, there were those in the Church who disagreed with him, but he believed firmly that the winds of change were blowing in the right direction. The Church couldn't get by forever with the old answers. That's why it was in so much trouble in the Third World, as well as here in the West. Pollution, environment—that was just another part of it.

But how? Pleased as he was to come to these conclusions, Father Lombardy still felt a bit weak about the physical nature of the thing. It would have to be incredible—well, it was, that was obvious. But could such a thing evolve from a complex mixture of organic compounds? Perhaps. He recognized that he simply didn't have the scientific knowledge to answer that, and he wondered if anyone did. But it was easy to imagine something bubbling up in a stagnant backwater of a swamp, something slowly but inexorably transformed by synthetic poisons, a science-fiction beast. Perhaps originally a bird of some kind, thus explaining its ability to move in the air. But its disappearing—that was harder still to accept. Unless… maybe it didn't disappear. He knew all too well from his own personal experience that the appearance of the thing occasioned great stress in the observer. So it could be that the thing only appeared to fade away, or materialize in thin air. The mind can play tricks; it could be nothing more than an optical illusion. That, combined with increased adrenal activity, could explain it.

Father Lombardy lit a cigarette with satisfaction. A look at his watch told him he hadn't smoked one in nearly forty minutes. He was on the way back out of the miasma of uncertainty and anguish.

But a new set of problems confronted him now. What to do about the thing. He should go to the police and tell them what he thought. But that could be embarrassing. He knew they were under siege from radio, TV and newspaper reporters, as well as special-interest groups such as the UFO-logists and occultists. If he went along with this theory they'd probably throw him out with the rest of the weirdoes. Father Lombardy went over the whole thing in his mind again and decided that it *was* entirely plausible. It wouldn't hurt to have the police check with scientists about the possibility, and also look into the chemical discharges from factories in the greater Waterbury area. Somebody could take the information and put it into a computer and come up with a probability factor, at least.

Still, the police angle worried him; not because he thought he might be wrong, but because he doubted his ability to penetrate their steel-plated skepticism. Maybe Father Connors—no, he wouldn't bring the old fart into it again. He would have to try the police, that's all there was to it, and if that didn't work he could go to—who? Perhaps someone at Yale or the University of Connecticut, a biologist or a biochemist.

It was a mystery now, difficult and dangerous, but a mystery on a human scale, back where it belonged. It could be solved.

The trees in the distance looked funny—greyish. No, bluish. Father Lombardy gasped and twisted his head—blue was settling on him! He stood up and tried to jump away, but it had him firmly in its grasp, surrounding him completely now. He struggled to keep his mind clear and free of panic. He could breathe, he could hear his own grunting, labored breathing, and he could still see things around him—though they were cast in drab monochrome. The thing seemed to have a million fingers picking at him and forcing him to the ground. No, both feet were just off the ground now, then touching lightly. He *could* barely move against the force, but it was like swimming in molasses. It was painful now, and his fear grew. He knew if he gave way to it he was lost, and he wouldn't accept that yet. He struggled desperately. If only he could tear loose and jump away, he could get a proper look at it. His face was pushed about and he could no longer see. What about the center, he thought? I missed it. He felt himself being turned in the air and pushed down to the ground sideways. He was losing, he knew. He sobbed violently and that used up more of his flagging energy. He felt the smooth, glassy surface of the foundation stones against his face and the pushing only increased. It was like he was in a hydraulic press now. He could barely open his mouth but he managed a last shriek, "No-o-o-o!" It couldn't happen now. He had to tell people. He knew, and he had to tell them. He knew.

Too late.

Early Monday morning Dave Corwin found Lombardy's car. He pushed it to the side of the dirt road, removed the barriers and drove up to the Mill. From the road he could see the body across the field on the grey stone. Corwin radioed in to the police station.

"Hey, we forgot one."

Lasker put his papers, wallet and recorder on the coffee-table. He kicked off his shoes and peeled the sweaty damp socks from his feet On his way into the kitchen he removed his shirt and let it drop to the floor. If this goes on much longer, he thought, I'll end up like Lutz, with my entire wardrobe scattered all over the place. He took a new quart carton of grape juice from the refrigerator and walked back into the living room. Still standing, he opened the container and took a long drink of the cool liquid. He bent over to place the carton on the table and completed the motion by falling heavily onto the sofa.

It had been another long day. Looking back on it, he found it difficult to think of anything useful he had done, but the running around, listening, talking—it was all more than enough to leave him dead tired. For a long time he remained sprawled out on the sofa without moving, eyes only half open. Finally he reached for the grape juice and took another large swallow. Some of it dribbled down his chin and onto his bare chest. It felt good, and the thought of a long cool shower suddenly appealed to him.

First, however, he had to go over his notes yet again. He picked up his note pad and turned to a clean white page. Let's start again. Somewhere it must connect, tie up. What am I missing? Only a brain. Keep going over it all until something comes through. He began to write a list of all the incidents he knew of that had taken place in the last couple of weeks. The same list he had stared at so many times before. He had the strange idea that a message might get through if he kept writing it out anew every day, like a schoolchild forced to write something out fifty or a hundred times.

He studied the list for several minutes, unable to find anything running through the items that would click, and so reveal something about the forces at work in the town. He flipped through his old notes looking for odd and irrelevant facts that might be juxtaposed into some kind of relevance. Twenty minutes later he had a few things that could only feed a paranoid fantasy. Still, he added them to his new list.

1.Bondarevsky:selling land for new development

2.School (Lutz): new building on old farm land

3.Pachman's Car: car

4. UFOs (Marge): seen near highway ext. & chemical plant

5. Donner: ?

6. Church Street: ? (old neighbor dying)

7. Library: ? (new building)

8. Richters: new apartment building

9. Field (Lutz): near new airport site

10. Mason's Mill: near new airport site

There was something in it, all right. A clammy feeling came over him and he was sure he was close to it. He would have to go downstairs and check in his old textbooks from the Classics course he had taken at college. Or maybe the encyclopedia would have it. It needed a lot more thought and confirmation, but it was there.

He was sure he knew.

PART THREE
THE FATES

"To-day grieves, tomorrow grieves,
Cover me over, light-in-leaves."
- T. S. Eliot

CHAPTER TEN

Jackie rocked back and forth distractingly, first putting her weight on her right leg, which was propped on the second step of the back porch, then leaning back on her left foot, which was planted firmly on the ground. Her hands were on her hips. Dave Lutz wondered if she was trying to look sexy or merely had to go to the bathroom. Perhaps it was a new kind of exercise. Whatever, it was pleasant to watch.

"Are you going to the Prom, Mr. Lutz?" the girl asked.

Lutz poured himself another vodka tonic, sipped it and said, "No. Once is enough in my life."

"Lots of the teachers go."

"That's their tough luck. Besides, you're only a sophomore, you won't be going to the Junior or Senior Prom."

"Yes, I will," Jackie smiled. "My boy-friend is a senior."

"What do all those poor sophomore boys do, go out with twelve-year-olds?"

"I can't help it if my boyfriend is two years older than I am." Jackie stopped her rocking and tucked her tee-shirt into her jeans, emphasizing her bust in the process.

Lutz had groaned to himself when the student walked along and dallied for a chat. He had just stretched out on the recliner on his back porch and a full pitcher of drink and a Philip K. Dick novel. Still, he had to admit Jackie was easy on the eyes.

"How can you worry about the Prom when the whole town is under siege from that thing, whatever it is?"

"There's nothing I can do about it, is there? I mean, if the police can't take care of it..." She finished the sentence with a shrug.

"True," he conceded.

"What do you think it is, Mr. Lutz?"

"One of Rilke's angels."

"Who's Rilke?"

"A poet who worried a lot."

"Oh." Jackie lost interest at the mention of something that might be school-work. But she couldn't quite let it go without checking. "Is he going to be in the final exam?"

"No."

"That's good."

"What do you think it is?" Lutz inquired.

"What?"

"The Millville monster."

"Oh. I don't know. My father says it's an electrical storm in the atmosphere caused by putting too many expensive satellites up in space."

"Really?"

"Yeah. Satellites weigh tons, you know, and he says all that metal up there does something with the electricity in the air and the result is what's happening in Millville. He says it could happen anywhere. He's mad, because he says that's what they do with the taxpayers' money. Cause trouble."

"Maybe he's right," Lutz said.

"Yeah? I think it's kinda dumb."

"Why?"

"How could satellites do that? I mean, it would have happened before now, wouldn't it?"

"Maybe. What do you think it is?" Lutz repeated the question pointedly. Why are these kids so slow to think for themselves?

"I don't know. I just wish it would stop."

Naturally, Lutz thought. The monster could pose a threat to the Prom.

The desultory conversation came to an end a few minutes later when Jackie looked at her watch, announced she had to meet friends and departed. Lutz watched her round bottom disappear up Sundrive Terrace and poured himself another drink. He picked up the novel, but after one paragraph he felt lazy and couldn't concentrate, so he put the book back on the side table.

Why am I always feeling so tired and lethargic, he wondered? Perhaps it's mononucleosis, he thought, but then discarded the idea. Unhealthy living—that's what it is. Too much drink, too much trashy instant food, depressing work, a disordered life style, lack of exercise—that was more than enough to account for it He would have to reform. He would have to give up drink—well, cut down considerably, a little, at least. Start eating good, natural, organic health foods; he could afford it. Take up some activity on a regular basis: swimming or walking or cycling. Clean up his apartment. The more he thought about it, the more repellent the whole notion seemed to him, and he took another large sip from the cool glass.

What was the point? His life wasn't going to change significantly anyhow, unless he got out of teaching—and he couldn't see that happening. He wasn't equipped to do any other kind of job, except unskilled labor, and that was out of the question. No, he would remain a teacher, all right. His grimmest vision was of himself in twenty more years, looking much the same as Bugs Belicki, the biology teacher he had had when he was a student at Millville High only a few years ago. Bugs was fat, bald, lecherous with the girl students, smoked like a fiend and probably drank too much. Lutz saw himself riding down the same street. Bugs died at the age of fifty-one, from coronary occlusion, the year before Lutz returned to Millville and took up teaching.

Well, that's crazy thinking, Lutz suddenly chastised himself. People get fat, bald, lecherous and become alcoholic ashtrays in any line of work. Teaching wasn't bad, as jobs went, in fact it was pretty damn good. The few good students who were genuinely interested, more than made up for the great majority who couldn't care less if Shakespeare happened to be a poet or a gerund. Life was like that.

What rankled was really the feeling that at the age of twenty-five Lutz was permanently wrapped up and consigned for the rest of his natural life. It all seemed to be over too quickly. "Twenty years of schooling and they put you on the day shift. Look out, kid," Bob Dylan had sung and the words came back to Lutz. He *shouldn't* feel so old, tired and settled, not now, not yet.

Perhaps some plan of modest reform was called for after all He could let himself go steadily to seed if he wanted to, just through neglect and inertia, but it wasn't necessary. For one thing, he should do something this summer, maybe take a trip to California, instead of sitting around on his butt for two months. Meet more people, do things. You have only yourself to blame if you become a sedentary fixture in Millville, he thought.

Lutz's considerations and the quiet evening were interrupted by the sound of breaking glass and shouting voices. He looked up Sundrive Terrace, but the street was deserted. The noise continued, increased even. Then a man rushed out from behind the shrubbery by the side of one house. He stopped briefly, looked over his shoulder and then began to run down the middle of the road in Lutz's direction. When he reached the building where Lutz sat, the man halted for a moment and then hollered, "They're coming! They're coming!" Then he ran off out of sight.

The noise up the street grew worse, and Lutz knew that the blue cloud had appeared again. But instead of growing anxious, or even physically leaving the scene, he almost burst out laughing. The man with his shouted warning had conjured up an absurd memory in Lutz's mind. In his third year at college Lutz's roommate was a business major named Howie Dilbert. They used to argue with each other at least once a week about the war in Vietnam. Lutz was against it, whereas Howie believed firmly that America had to be in there fighting. The North Vietnamese were, after all, only doing the dirty work for their power-mad Chicom paymaster ('Moe-Say Toon'). But it didn't stop there, because the Kremlin was involved too. Whenever Lutz said America should withdraw its troops, Howie Dilbert would say, "Leonard Breshnof would love you." The reason the man running down Sundrive Terrace in Millville, obviously in a state of terror, reminded Lutz of Howie, was because his former roommate believed that Vietnam was only the first step. If America didn't stop them there, the North Vietnamese would overrun Australia and soon be landing on the beaches of California, at which point Howie might well set off like a latter-day Paul Revere, warning, "They're coming!"

Where was Howie Dilbert now? Lutz wondered. Safe and snug and prosperous somewhere, no doubt Still worrying about 'them'?

The blue cloud emerged from the same yard from which the running man had fled. It chewed up grass, branches from trees, flowers, shingles from the side of the house, destroying and spitting out everything it came into contact with. A car came around the bend further up the road, jammed on its brakes and reversed quickly, veering wildly as it did so. The blue cloud drifted down the street, ripping up chunks of asphalt from the road, tearing loose a mailbox and sending it crashing into a nearby house.

It did make a noise, Lutz thought, wondering why he hadn't noticed it at Mason's Mill. Too concerned about that girl. That was a mistake, she had only been polite to him anyhow.

People came out of their houses and scurried up the street, away from the blue cloud. It just went anywhere, Lutz noticed. It didn't seek people out—well, it did at the Mill. But now it seemed to move aimlessly, not going out of its way to attack people, not avoiding them, just moving. An aleatoric phenomenon.

Then it slowed, hovered in front of a house for a few moments. The group of people who had left their houses stopped about a hundred yards up the street, watching. The same terrified fascination, Lutz thought. He felt it too. He should move, get the hell out of there, but he wanted to stay as long as he could, to see if the thing was actually going to come in his direction. It was slow enough to avoid if it did. And if it didn't, why should he move?

The cloud took up the picket fence in front of the house and spun it to pieces, shooting off the white-painted boards in all directions. One landed with a clatter on the sidewalk near Lutz's building. The thing continued to work on the same spot, now prying loose chunks of cement and turf.

If I imagined one of Rilke's angels from *The Duino Elegies*, that is how it would look, Lutz thought. In his impassioned youth, five or six decades ago it seemed, he had learned whole passages by heart. Now the opening lines of the sequence came back to him.

Who, if I cried, would hear me among the angelic orders? And even if one of them suddenly pressed me against his heart, I should fade in the strength of his stronger existence. For Beauty's nothing but beginning of Terror we're still just able to bear, and why we adore it so is because it serenely disdains to destroy us. Every angel is terrible.

But these angels do destroy, Lutz thought, as the blue light moved down the street in his direction. There is no angelic order. No stronger existence. Of that, Lutz was certain. He had gone through his mystical phase years ago, and recovered completely.

But this thing was something else. Why had people said it was a burning light? Lutz could see no burning, throbbing fire at the center of it In fact, the thing hardly even looked blue, more a wash of drab grey, thick and opaque, streaked with reddish brown, the blue virtually gone. Close up it was almost dull, and would be dull if it were not so clearly out of the ordinary. Like the dull grey he saw in the morning, every morning, shifting color variations on the same theme. Endless dead blah.

Suddenly Lutz understood what it was that he was looking at. It wasn't just the strange cloud of energy come down to kill and destroy. He was looking at his own life, his future as he feared it might be. He could see now that other people had failed to grasp this one simple point about the apparition: everyone perceived it as something different, something particular, something tied fatefully to their own individual selves. It was both an attack on, and a mirror to, each person who confronted it, a challenge. Where they had failed was as a group in their perception of the thing.

First the Marianists, who wanted to see the Virgin Mary come down to earth before man. With a message. Then the people like Marge Calder, who wanted to believe they were seeing another, more advanced civilization, perhaps one that could help man. And the people like the police chief, who saw it as a threat to their own positions, something to be refuted, crushed. Doctor Acevedo, the antique academic who believed it was his mythology come to life. The man from Colorado whose letter appeared in the newspaper today, saying that Millville was one of the few special places on the planet, a "favored zone" he had called it, where the magnetic, radionic and topographic (whatever they were) forces were most powerful— getaways to another dimension, or from an alternate universe. And all the other people with their own peculiar ideas and explanations—

everyone was seeing something of themselves in the blue cloud, some essential cornerstone of their thinking and being.

Maybe the irony was even greater. Maybe, Lutz, thought, my prime blockhead Nardello wasn't so far off when he said it was a kind of mass hysteria or hallucination. Real, yes. Independent and autonomous, yes. But also part of the minds of the people of Millville. Something that appeared from who knows where and then began to grow, fed by the collective psyche of the townspeople, a mad, hopeless confusion of warring identities.

Lutz stood and stared into the heart of the looming monster. It was coming very close now, but he knew he had to stand and face it. He had to see if he was there, in it, and if it was a part of him. As he feared it was. If he saw nothing but the blindness of a vacuum, a void, he could move, turn away, leave. But if he saw…

The cloud sheared along the pavement into the hedge, sending up a shower of twigs and leaves and bits of concrete. It cut a slow swath along the edge of the yard, but did not come any closer to the porch on which Lutz stood trembling. His eyes widened with awe at the enormity of the thing this close. But it was moving down the street. Yes, it was going to pass the house. It would not touch him, he could see that now, and he felt his heart pounding and his blood racing as he tingled all over with fear and—joy! *I've won*, he thought, *I've won! I was right, I've beaten it!*

He turned to watch it pass, exultant as bits of hedge and pebbles bounced off him. Then the white, pointed picket from the scattered fence up the street was sucked into the cloud and then hurled out at great velocity, impaling Lutz in the center of his chest.

Yes! his mind screamed.

———

"Isn't that the most pathetic thing you ever saw?" Ned Hanley stared into the distance for a long minute. He worked up a hefty slob of saliva and phlegm in his mouth and then spat it out. He felt a small flicker of satisfaction as it splattered loudly in the gutter. Seven feet in the air, at least, he reckoned. Haven't done that since I was a kid, when I used to do it ten or fifteen times a day.

Chief Sturdevent glanced briefly at Hanley with distaste, then his gaze returned to the farce being acted out a quarter of a mile away in the vast parking lot of the Pioneer Shopping Plaza. "It won't work," he muttered.

"They might as well try pissing on it," Hanley agreed cheerfully.

Three trucks—the entire Millville Fire Department—were triangularly positioned at a safe distance around the pillar of fire. The men had edged as close to the thing as they dared and were spraying hundreds of gallons of water on it. From where Hanley and Sturdevent stood, this action produced an attractive little rainbow, but had no visible effect on the target.

At first the scene had looked fascinating, but now Sturdevent found it only foolish. Well, it was the Mayor's idea, and they all should have known better than to think it might work, but of course they were obliged to give it a try. At a tense and heated meeting of town authorities Mayor Sherwin had argued that everything should be tried against the Millville terror. Fair enough. His own theory, which Sturdevent knew to have been lifted whole from a newspaper article, was that the thing might well prove to be a kind of fireball. Everyone said, didn't they, that it had a burning, glowing center. Didn't that one in the parking lot now look just like a huge torch of pale white flame? Wasn't it possible, then, that the thing could be extinguished as easily as a cigarette? Just turn on the water? Mayor Sherwin had read a book called *War of the Worlds*, in which Martians are destroyed by the common cold. That was fiction, of course, but the lesson it demonstrated was nonetheless valid, and in the face of Millville's present circumstances it would be irresponsible not to try any means to overcome this foe. So now Millville firemen were out there risking their lives and looking stupid to boot. Sturdevent was disgusted. The whole town was going crazy. Slowly and even calmly, but crazy all the same.

The police station foyer was crammed every day now with quacks and fruitcakes from all over the country, each with his or her own prescription for salvation. The Kinetic Displacement theory. The Trencher Society. The Rhomboid Revitalists. Doctor Bender's theory of Reverse Blindspots. And the occultists who wanted to bring in an army of three hundred. They would sit down on the ground in a huge circle around the monster and concentrate until they had banished the evil presence from Millville's astral territory, or some such thing. Sturdevent had shuddered with visions of another Mason's Mill when he heard that suggestion. Besides, he didn't trust people like that. More than likely they had some ulterior motive. The entire nut brigade.

Hanley heard the car radio squawk and he went over to answer it.

Sturdevent shifted his weight on his feet. The damn thing probably likes all that water, he thought blackly. The fire-cloud began to move at its now familiar slow but deliberate pace. The firemen dropped their hoses and scattered quickly, although they weren't in any danger of being overtaken. The people of Millville had learned a few things about the monster. Sometimes it could be avoided, if you moved away quickly and didn't panic. The real danger was when it appeared within a room or any enclosed space. Then—forget it. That was what happened most of the time now. The death toll was rising.

Hanley returned and said that another blue cloud had appeared downtown.

"Corwin says the area's pretty well cleared, but I'm going to get over there."

"Okay," Sturdevent replied.

"You want to come?"

"No, I'll stay and keep an eye on this one."

"You'll have to walk back to the office."

"I know," Sturdevent snapped.

"Okay." Hanley got into the police car and drove away.

That was another thing. The monster was actually several monsters, or else it was capable of splitting itself into separate units. They were beginning to pop up all over Millville, like mushrooms, some big, some small. Some like clouds, some like fire, some a mixture of both. Sometimes like ghostly figures. And in different colors. As small as a car or as large as a barn. But in whatever form it turned up, it was always deadly.

He'd had enough. The notion that he and his family might pack up and leave had simmered just below the surface of his consciousness for the past week. Now it had broken through into the open light of day.

The light. This was a decent town once, a good place to work and raise kids. Not now, not anymore.

Sturdevent was standing on the raised ground of the railroad bed. Two tracks wide. Millville was a small town. Below, and in the distance, the fire-cloud rolled into the gaudy front of The Dive Inn, an instant food restaurant, spewing out plastic and chrome. Good enough, Sturdevent nodded, I never did like that place. Knock it down.

Yes, he would have to talk to Jean about it. He knew she wouldn't like the idea, but he thought he would be able to persuade her. Millville wasn't safe anymore. The kids wouldn't like the idea either, and that was understandable. They had all their friends here, and other attachments, like the Little League, but that was too bad. It's easier for the young to adjust to change anyhow, he thought. It'll be harder on Jean and me. Much harder.

Selling the house was going to be a bitch, that was for sure. Who would want to buy a home in a town with a half-dozen monsters floating around? Maybe a rich crackpot seeking adventure? Anyhow, he had some money set aside for the kids' college education and he could use that until such time as the house was sold, and if he got a job right away in another police department—in a position below that of chief, probably, unfortunately—then they would be all right. The fact that he had come from Millville might even work to his advantage, in a way. It was an impossible situation, no one would dispute that. He might even be something of a minor celebrity. They had shown part of his press conference on state-wide television, after all; he hadn't looked too good, but that might earn him a little sympathy.

Sturdevent was almost certain he would leave. Even if these things went away tomorrow, he no longer wanted to remain in Millville. Too much shit, shit, shit, with every two-bit creep in town, from Hanley to Sherwin to the people of the *Millville News*. They were sticking it to him from every direction. At a time like this you'd think they'd all be pulling together to try to make it through the trouble. But no, they were falling apart, each man trying to cover his own ass and do in his neighbor at the same time. He at least had made his plea. He had stood up in front of all those people and asked them to work together, to help rather than hinder their efforts to survive this nightmare. He didn't have to put himself on the line like that, but he did. What for? All he got was more shit. Sherwin screaming like a baby that Sturdevent had attacked the free press and made Millville sound like a funny farm. He had said just the opposite, but Sherwin was so far gone he couldn't see that. He just wanted to ram another blade in Sturdevent.

The fire-cloud had drifted out of the Plaza now and was floating along the street into town. It would pass under the railroad trestle if it stayed on its present course. If it swerves up here, I'm done, Sturdevent thought. He still had the heavy Ace bandage wrapped around his ankle and he had to walk carefully, although the small fracture was healing nicely and causing no pain. But I won't be able to run if I have to, he thought. It didn't bother him, however, as some instinct told him the thing would roll on by.

In the street below, the fire-cloud moved along slowly, bending a tall metal street-light in its way. Nobody has noticed that it never seems to tear down the electricity wires, Sturdevent thought. Is that significant? Maybe it doesn't like electricity. I ought to drop that little titbit in Sherwin's ear and watch him try to figure out ways of electrocuting the monster. That was his kind of idea. Bastard.

That was another thing. Sturdevent noticed that his language was getting rougher. He had prided himself on not talking garbage. A police chief wasn't supposed to talk that way, and he had been good at watching his words. But now, since this business started up, he was thinking and talking more and more in the foul language of people like Hanley. That annoyed him a great deal, because it was one more example of how they were breaking him down, working on him. The next thing, he'd go home and say shit or fuck in front of the kids. He would leave Millville before things got to that point.

The blue cloud rolled under the trestle, exactly as Sturdevent had expected. It just touched the railroad ties through the open lattice-work of the steel structure. Sturdevent watched as the girders buckled ever so slightly under the enormous stress. The thick wooden ties were pulled and then snapped downwards. Jesus, that thing is strong. There was no immediate danger of a train crash; the few trains that did call in to, or pass through, Millville had already been re-routed, voluntarily, by Conrail.

The damn thing is going to mosey right down the street, Sturdevent thought, as the fire-cloud continued along on its way. He hopped, on his good foot, down the path along the side of the railroad embankment and made his way cautiously into Brunswick Street. There it was, large as life. Larger. Sturdevent stood about half a block behind the menace as it moved away from him. He walked along, keeping pace with it — about twenty yards a minute, he judged, faster than he had ever seen it before. It was steering a course down the middle of the street, not touching the buildings or even the parked cars on either side. As if it were out for a walk, on its best behavior. Does it have a mind? Sturdevent had to watch his step, as the roadway was gouged and cut. He didn't want to twist or fall on his mending ankle.

Nobody around, nobody at all, he noticed. People were faster now at getting out of the way. Way out of the way. Where did they all go he wondered? Maybe into the ground, into those old fall-out shelters that had been all the rage back twenty years ago or so. Plenty of Sturdevent's friends had spent a lot of money having their back gardens dug out and fall-out shelters installed. Every day back then it seemed there was going to be a nuclear war. The canned-food business must have cleaned up. He had never given in to the temptation to buy one of those shelters. Screw it, if that kind of war comes, who'd want to live? Who'd want to live in a steel box ten feet under the petunia patch anyhow? Maybe the people in Millville who had fall-out shelters were using them now, finally getting their return on investment, finally opening up those cans of beans. And maybe they'll die of food poisoning while hiding from the monster. What a world, Sturdevent sighed.

The cloud stopped and hovered, as if to make up its mind, at the street corner up ahead. Sturdevent stopped too. He put his right hand on his hip, waiting patiently for something to happen, and felt the rounded sides of the bullets in the police holster around his waist. He hadn't worn a gun in years but he had taken his revolver out of the locker last week. Things were getting hairy in Millville and it might be necessary to have a gun at hand. Now he took the revolver out and hefted it, twice only, in his hand. A .357 magnum, regulation police issue. In twenty-three years as a policeman he had never had occasion to use the gun. In a small town like this you might go through your entire life without having to unstrap it, let alone fire a shot. In a small town like this. Like this was.

Sturdevent clicked off the safety and raised the revolver. Should use two hands, he thought, but his left hand was still in a cast from being broken at Mason's Mill. He levelled the barrel of the revolver, fixing its sight at the center fire-cloud. He squeezed the trigger and the noise was much louder than he had anticipated. His wrist hurt from the powerful recoil. It would have been nice if the monster had collapsed in a gassy heap on the street, or even disappeared in a puff, but Sturdevent knew that bullets were of no use against the thing. Plenty of people around town had been taking pot-shots at the cloud for the last two weeks now. That's why Sturdevent had dusted off his own pistol—for protection against the locals. Now he had fired the gun just to see what it was like after so long. Not bad. A symbolic protest.

He raised the heavy weapon and fired. Again. Again. Again. Even as the reports echoed in his ears he could make out the distant sound of breaking glass. But the cloud hadn't moved. Sturdevent stepped over to the side of the street, and then further, against a building, until he could see around the edge of the fire-cloud. Yes, there it was—a broken window in a building on the far side of the T-intersection. His shots had gone right through the cloud. He realized he could have hit, even killed someone standing in the room behind that window, but the thought didn't especially worry him. Anybody standing there would be half crazy anyhow. Like most of the people in Millville.

After a brief interval the cloud began to move again, turning right at the corner. It brushed against the building at the turn, the offices of a local insurance agency. Sturdevent held back as the glass doors and windows exploded in millions of tiny, deadly bits of flying shrapnel. Slimy bastards, he grinned, serves you right. Knock it all down. He had insurance and he hated it. House, car, theft, fire, and of course life. Conning people into betting on their own deaths. Venetian blinds flew through the air like surreal accordions tangled, twisted, and broken. Sturdevent followed the cloud around the corner, wondering if Ribault & McGrath had insured themselves. What would you call this? An act of God? Vandalism? Could you take out a policy against the unknown?

Sturdevent had to stand back again, as the fire-cloud proceeded along a row of storefronts, filling the immediate vicinity with a spray of debris. He used the time to reload his revolver.

A man ran into the street from one of the partially wrecked shops the fire-cloud had just passed. He looked at the monster and then began to run. He immediately saw Sturdevent and yelled, "Police!"

Bright guy, Sturdevent thought. "Get the hell out of here, mister," he roared, resenting the man's intrusive presence. He wanted to be alone out here in what had been his town. Alone with the thing.

The man kept running, right on by Sturdevent and around the corner, out of sight.

No cars on the road. The last stranger gone. To Chief Sturdevent it looked like a stage set, no—a Hollywood film set. He had seen the streets of Millville deserted before on many occasions, early in the morning, late at night or even at supper-time. It was that kind of town. Had been. Now he could see for the first time that it tried too hard, like a film set or children's toys, and ended up being less than real The whole place had a thrown-together look about it. Cheap dumpy little shops, tired brick buildings, ugly gas stations. Plastic. Glass. Junk. Why had he never noticed that hollowness before? What's happening to me?

The fire-cloud swung back into the street again and Sturdevent quickened his pace to restore the smaller gap between them. As he walked he emptied the revolver into the heart of the beast again. The gun was hot in his hand and his fingers ached to let go of the heavy weapon. He paused, awkwardly, to reload. Bullets didn't hurt the thing but maybe he was actually prodding it along, making it move just a little bit quicker. See more of the sights of Millville. He had to admit he was almost fond of the monster now. It had ruined his life, sure, and the lives of many other people as well. But he could come through it a changed man and maybe that wasn't altogether a bad thing. He wasn't too old to move, to change. One thing was for sure, he wouldn't look at cute and cozy towns through the same rose-colored glasses anymore. He had learned to look at everything in a different way now. A lot more realistically.

He slammed the chambers of the gun shut against his thigh, lifted it and fired again. A second shot. Take it easy. Reloading is a clumsy business with only one good hand. How many bullets did they put on one of these belts? — a lot, he saw, in case you happened across a small regional war.

Sturdevent angled from one side of the street to the other, peering beyond the nebulous fringe of the cloud. Then he took two quick steps forward, set himself, aimed carefully and fired through the center of the pale thing. He was again rewarded with the sound of shattering glass — a car parked about a hundred feet beyond. The gaping hole in the windscreen was on the passenger side but that didn't bother Sturdevent. A hit was what counted.

The cloud swung into another corner and tore down a large part of the building situated there, this time a two-story brick structure containing offices. The front rooms collapsed in a heap of rubble, furniture and billowing dust. No work for you folks tomorrow, Sturdevent smirked, following the fire-cloud.

From the corner, standing among the crumbled bricks and broken chairs, with the dust still swirling thickly, he got off two good angle shots through the cloud, demolishing the neon sign in the distance that had said Mel's Radio & TV.

On they went, maintaining the same distance between them, moving at the same sluggish pace, up one street and down another, slowly circling in towards the center of town.

Sturdevent wondered if they were going to meet up with the other cloud they had heard about. That would be a new development.

He had four bullets left in his belt when the cloud abruptly faded and then vanished completely. He was hot and tired and his body felt sore all over. He sat on the edge of the sidewalk and placed the hot revolver on the ground to cool off. A thought entered his mind. I wasn't prodding it, not at all. On the contrary, it was leading me, leading me through my own town. As if to say, See.

What was my town.

What was left of it.

What had been my town.

Leading me.

Saying: here you are.

Here I am.

Any other town seemed very far away.

Here you are.

Nearly an hour later Ned Hanley, cruising the streets, came across a figure he recognized. He stopped his car and got out. Christ, he must have walked here from the plaza.

Sturdevent was slumped over on the curb. Has he shot himself, Hanley suddenly wondered? No, Sturdevent isn't that brave. He's finished, that's for sure. He just doesn't know it yet. One of the walking dead. Hanley felt nothing but contempt.

He bent over and lifted up Sturdevent's head. Glassy eyes, looking dopey. What a useless wreck. There were grimy smear marks on the Chiefs face, as if he had been sweating a great deal, or crying.

"Martin. How nice to see you. Come in." Marge Calder smiled warmly and held the aluminum screen door open for him.

"Thanks," Lasker said, entering the house. I hope I didn't pick a bad time to stop by."

"Not at all. I'm glad you did."

They walked into the living room.

"You're looking great," he told her. "How do you feel now? All better?"

"All right, thanks, but I'm still taped up in places." She smiled sheepishly. "Can I get you something to drink?"

"Lemonade?"

"I have some, yes, but would you like something a little stronger?"

"No, lemonade would be fine, thanks."

"Okay. Sit down, make yourself comfortable."

Lasker watched her walk into the adjoining kitchen. Her brightly-colored caftan didn't entirely hide the layers of bandages wrapped around her torso underneath and her movements were stiff. At Mason's Mill she too had been caught in the crush of the panicking crowd. In addition to numerous cuts and bruises, including a gruesome black eye that had now completely disappeared, she had suffered two cracked ribs and a concussion.

"When did you get out of the hospital?" Lasker asked, standing in the archway between the two rooms.

"I was only in for a couple of days."

"That's good."

"Yes," she agreed, handing him a tall glass of iced lemonade. "But I've been stuck here ever since. Doctor's orders not to go out until the bones are fully mended."

They sat down in the living room.

"That makes sense," Lasker said.

"Yes, but I'm beginning to feel like a prisoner in my own home. I can't wait to get out. It's good of you to stop in and visit. I was almost ready to start talking to myself."

"You make good lemonade." Lasker smiled.

"It comes from a can." She smiled back.

"You shouldn't have told me."

"What's been happening with you? I haven't been keeping up on the news but you must be very busy with everything that's going on."

"Well, yes and no. At the moment, I'm unemployed," he admitted.

"Really?" Her eyes widened slightly. "How come?"

"It's not like it sounds. The other night one of the monsters appeared on the scene and wrecked the presses. So the paper is out of action, and so am I, at least for the time being. They haven't made up their minds what they're going to do."

"That's terrible. Was anyone hurt? I didn't hear about it on the radio, but then I've almost given up listening now. It's all bad news."

"Right. Nobody was seriously injured. It was very late and most of the staff had gone home already. The despatchers were able to get away without much trouble."

"That's something."

"They may have the paper printed in Waterbury until they can repair the damage and get new machines in, so I might be back at work in a few days. But they have problems—whether or not all that costly equipment is covered by insurance, and so on. Nobody knows what's going to happen."

"I heard about the National Guard and the Army."

"Yeah, better late than never, I guess."

"Will they be able to do anything?"

"I doubt it." Lasker gulped the lemonade, draining the glass. "Help evacuate people is the main thing."

"Want some more?"

"Uh-okay."

She returned in a few seconds with the pitcher of lemonade.

"Thanks," Lasker said.

"What do you think will happen?"

"It'll just keep getting worse, as far as I can see. It's bad enough now with people being killed every day, the enormous property damage being done. Ordinary life has ground to a halt. Either this plague will go away or the entire town will be steadily wiped out."

"Do you fed afraid?"

"Strangely enough, I don't, although I guess I should. They seem to be all over the place now." Lasker wanted to get away from this subject. The real reason he felt no fear about the monsters was the death of his friend, Dave Lutz. That tragic event had aged Lasker in some deep but unfathomable way. He felt no anger or bitterness and he could not fear the thing. He knew only the desolation of a void in his heart. He felt nothing. He didn't want to talk about it.

"I don't feel afraid either." Marge's eyes were bright and lively. "I did at first, in the hospital when I was reacting to the injuries and the sight of the thing close up at the Mill. I was afraid then. Stu wanted us to leave, go stay with his parents in Pennsylvania until this thing was over, but then I decided I wanted to stay. The fear went, I don't know why, and I wanted to stay here. This is my house."

Lasker nodded. He was beginning to think this visit wasn't such a great idea. All conversations in Millville were now gloomy and morbid.

"At least your husband knows now you weren't seeing neon lights." He tried to raise a smile.

"Yes, but I feel bad about that."

"Why?"

"I should have made more noise at the time. Alerted people to what was out there, instead of worrying about how silly I might look and waiting until things really got bad."

"Not at all," Lasker said firmly. "You had no way of knowing what those things would turn out to be. Nobody did. Besides, no one would have paid any attention to you. And you did tell me about it and I didn't know what to make of it."

"Maybe." She was willing to be convinced.

"People are like that. They have to see for themselves before they believe, especially something as fantastic as this." He poured his third glass of lemonade. "If anyone should feel responsible it's me. On two counts."

"Why?"

"Because I'm a news reporter, at least I'm supposed to be, and I could have done something. I've gone through this whole disaster like a blind person, never seeing exactly what was happening and what it was leading up to, missing every connection from that damn cow onwards. I couldn't get a hold of it and come to terms with it." Lasker sighed unhappily. "The other thing is, I shouldn't have suggested you go out to Mason's Mill that day. That was just stupid of me and it nearly got you killed."

"I was the one who behaved stupidly," she said quickly, touched by his remark. "Not you. I went of my own free will. Don't blame yourself. I had these dizzy, dreamy notions—God, I feel so foolish now, I was like a child. I thought I was going to see something... I don't know." She couldn't bring herself to mention flying saucers again.

"Anyhow, it's all rolling under its own steam now," Lasker said. "Millville is big news now. Midsummer madness."

"Has anyone found out what those things are, or come up with an idea? I mean an idea that might be right. I've heard about some of the others."

Lasker shrugged dispiritedly. "Waterbury is full of weathermen at the moment. The idea they're working on is that it all has something to do with meteorological disturbances in connection with sunspot activity, or something like that."

"Well, they won't be able to do much about that if it turns out to be the case. Will they?"

"No, they won't. But the idea is a very popular one. There's a story going around that it prompted Mayor Sherwin to ask the state congressman from our district, a fellow named Bronson, to ask the Governor to ask Washington to look into the possibility that the Russians may be trying out some new kind of weather-control weapon on us."

"Oh," Marge replied, not responding to Lasker's thin sarcasm.

"But they're all wrong. Very wrong."

"Do you think so?"

"Yes, I do," Lasker said with quiet certainty. "I've been slow in coming to it, as I said before, but I think I've finally put it all together."

"Tell me," Marge said, leaning back in her chair.

"Very simply, it's this. We've been violating the natural order of life in countless ways and what has been happening here is a kind of retaliation. And a warning to us. A demonstration by Nature or God or whatever you want to call it. The ancient Greeks called them the Fates, the daughters of Night. There *is* a natural order to things and man has been violating it. Millville has been made an example, by the Fates if you like, to show us that we have to restore and maintain that natural order."

"I'm not sure I'm following you," Marge said with a sympathetic but confused look.

"Bondarevsky was the first. He's been selling his land so people can stick up ugly apartment blocks and offices. The car that was destroyed. Church Street—a neighborhood that has been dying slowly for years. Mason's Mill is due to become part of the new airport complex. The gathering of the people there—for what, if not to teach them a lesson? Can you see what ties it all together?"

"The environment?"

"Yes, Nature."

"But there isn't much real pollution in Millville, except out by the Gunntown factory."

"Which was levelled yesterday afternoon."

"Really?"

"Yeah. I'm telling you. I know I'm right."

"I see," Marge said, still sounding unimpressed. "Are you going to write all that up in the newspaper—when it gets going again—listing the incidents and all?"

"I don't know," Lasker replied. He hoped that Phipps would run such a story but he was not at all certain the editor would. He might consign it to the bulging file of crank theories. Lasker also caught the irony of Marge's question. When he first met her he was the one who listened with polite skepticism to her story. Now the situation had been reversed.

He roused himself and sat forward in the large, soft chair, making a show of looking at his watch. "I should go."

"Oh, why don't you stay for lunch?" Marge suggested. "You said you're not working and I enjoy company."

"Well... I am still following up various things, but..." He left the sentence unfinished. He would have to eat at some point, but on the other hand he didn't feel very conversational. He sat poised and silent in a state of indecision.

"Come on," Marge prodded. "I'll make you a delicious fat submarine sandwich."

Is that a Freudian slip, Lasker wondered hopefully? "Sounds wonderful."

"Good."

She went into the kitchen. Lasker slumped back in the chair and watched her moving about. Why hadn't he made a pass at her before? Now he could entertain the idea as much as he liked but he couldn't do anything about it until she had recovered from her injuries. Still... you never knew. The other time—he should have tried it the other time he had been here. He liked her because she didn't pretend to be someone she wasn't—the way she had reacted to his Greek mythology, for instance. And she was an attractive young woman. As she stood in the kitchen he pictured her as she had been that other day, in white shorts and a clinging top. A missed opportunity, or was he just kidding himself? Lasker the hesitant lover.

She turned her back to him and the sunlight streaming in through the bay window by the kitchen table shone through her thin summery caftan, making shadows of her long, slender legs. They're good legs all right, Lasker thought. Then the light changed slightly and her legs disappeared behind the cloth and she turned to the cabinet for something.

It took Lasker several seconds to realize that the light had changed before she had turned, ending his brief reverie. The light. As if a cloud had passed in front of the sun.

Light.

Cloud.

He slowly got to his feet, turned and looked out the living room picture window. Greyish swirls. Like fog. At last the message reached his brain.

"Come on," he said, hurrying to her. "Come on, now."

She looked at him blankly for a second and then at the window. "Oh my God. No, oh no."

Lasker grabbed her arm but he didn't know where to go. The kitchen window, the dining room window—everywhere was the same greyish veil. A cloud was settling on the house. Then a painfully loud rending noise came from over their heads and the floor shuddered beneath their feet.

"The cellar," he said. "Where is the cellar door?"

Marge continued to look around, a horrified expression on her face.

Lasker shook her. "Where's the damn cellar? We have to get down there, now come on."

"Around there." She pointed and Lasker immediately pulled her along the hallway to the door. "It won't do any good," she continued, her voice a high-pitched tremor.

"Yes, it will," Lasker insisted.

He shut the door behind them and flicked all the switches mounted on the wall. Lights came on. Four steps down. A typical shallow modern basement, he thought unhappily. The house in which he had grown up had a proper deep cellar, at least twelve steps down, well into the earth. Not one of these. This was almost as bad as being in one of the rooms upstairs.

The noise from above increased. Some of the tools which Stuart Calder had put up on a plywood panel on one wall now slipped from their places and clanked on the concrete floor.

Lasker stood looking around helplessly, still clutching Marge's arm above the wrist tightly. He felt foolish and angry. Angry with himself.

He had squandered his time and now he was trapped. Too much time thinking, dreaming, head in the—clouds.

Marge was weeping silently as the din around them grew steadily worse. The lights flickered and held. But not for much longer, Lasker knew.

He let go of her arm and rushed to the other cellar door, which led up into the back yard. He slid back the flimsy supermarket bolt and opened the door. The hatchway a few steps up was heavy metal. He didn't believe it could withstand the force of the cloud but it was the only chance they had. The empty space, smaller than a closet, behind the open steps. If they could get in there they might just survive. Like worms caught in the bottom of a tin can, he thought bitterly. He tested the wooden planks. They were thick, solid and heavy. The entire stairway had been built right into the concrete of the foundation. If he could remove just one step they might slide in—and pray their wood and cement pocket didn't become their coffin. He checked that the steel bolts on the hatchway were securely in place and then looked around Stuart's workbench for something to break loose a step with.

Marge backed against the wall. She wasn't crying now. She seemed oblivious to Lasker, the infernal racket above and the first trembling of the basement as the Calder house shook in the grip of the monster.

Gone.

Her house.

Gone.

The word floated randomly like a bubble in her mind. Gone, all gone.

Lasker took a hammer, the first potentially useful implement he came across, and began to pound on one of the steps, but immediately saw it wouldn't work. The fat beams had been screwed down into the frame—of course—which meant he would have to swing the hammer upwards to knock the screws loose. An impossible task that close to the floor and with so little time.

Stupid, stupid, stupid, he thought feverishly as he tossed the hammer aside and rummaged about for something else. The ceiling began to groan, then lit up slightly. The lights went out as cables, pipes and insulation were ripped loose. The only light reaching the basement now came from the tiny window at ground level above the workbench. Water sprayed from a broken copper pipe and feathery green tufts of fireproof insulating material sifted down through the air.

Lasker found a small axe and he started chopping frenziedly at the bottom step. It was hard going. "Fucking boy scout axe," he said aloud. The air around him was now a blizzard of dust and insulation. Then one side of the step was done, hacked through crudely. Lasker didn't bother to start chopping the other side. He threw the axe away and sat down on the floor beside the stairs, bracing his back against the concrete doorway. With both hands he pushed the loose end of the step up and away. It gave, grudgingly. As soon as there was room enough he propped his feet against the underside of the plank and pushed. A few good kicks and finally the beam tore loose, falling to the floor. Lasker quickly rolled under the second step—yes, they would fit. The stairway was maybe five feet wide and the same again in depth.

The floorboards above were coming loose now, snapping and tearing with horrible shrieking noises. As if the cloud is showing me it can do the same thing with no effort at all, Lasker thought. Not necessary. I know.

He got to his feet, shouting for Marge, but he could hardly hear his own words. Where the hell was she? He groped around awkwardly, half-blind with the dust and material that swirled everywhere and clogged his watery eyes. Then he saw her a few feet away, grabbed her arm and made for the stairwell. But she was resisting, shaking her head.

"It's our only chance," he screamed in her ear.

"I don't want to die in there like that," she answered.

Neither do I, he thought. Neither in there nor out here. Six-and ten-foot floorboards now began to drop around them from above. Lasker didn't bother to say anything more to her. He yanked her by the arm to the stairwell and was surprised to find that her resistance ended suddenly. He motioned with his hands and she got down on the floor and slid under the steps. He followed. Then he reached out through the open planks and pulled the inside cellar door shut. It was made of quarter-inch thick plywood slats; a healthy teenager, Lasker knew, could kick through it without any difficulty. But he wanted it closed so

Marge wouldn't have to see her home and possessions crashing down into the cellar.

He couldn't see her in the dark. He felt around with his hands, found her feet and placed them against the lower step. He found her ear and told her to brace her back against the concrete wall, keeping her feet firmly on the step. When she did so, he set himself in the same manner.

Like we're riding on a sled, he thought, in a dusty snow. Sliding into nowhere.

That was no good. He had *not to think*. The Fates had come. For him. For her. For everyone. That was all. He didn't want to die thinking of his childhood or of his family or friends, those already dead and those living for the present. He didn't want to think of anything at all. There was nothing left to think of.

All he could do was open his ears completely to the monstrous sounds that assaulted them, open his burning eyes to the dust and dim shapes, feel the nervous ungodly shiver of wood and cement and earth, taste the grit and hot choking air... Feel the lines of Marge's body huddled against him in the dark... Inhale the rising fetor...

No, she thought. That was the word: no. She could feel the vibration of the sound along her facial bones but not hear it.

No.

No.

No.

Her side ached sharply, the two ribs probably refractured, she realized. What an irrelevant thought. My house. My home. To die like slime.

Even if it goes away.

Even if we live.

We're dead.

———

The door rattled.

EPILOGUE

Joe Garfield sat on his front porch.

For the first time in weeks there was a breeze in the air. The kind of cool summer evening breeze that made the maple leaves sing gently in the trees and brought the smell of freshly-mown grass up the street. It was the first pleasant evening since that whole trouble started with Ernie Pachman's car. Maybe it would even rain. That would be good.

Joe had another sip of beer. Yes, it was finished—all that trouble. There hadn't been any more appearances or attacks in town for ten days or so, maybe longer. It seemed to have ended. But the absence of the thing was only part of it. There was also a feeling in the air, a feeling as tangible as this lovely breeze. People were beginning to come out of hiding at last—those who had stayed in Millville—and those who had fled were drifting back cautiously. The patient was still sick but the fever had passed, the devastation ended.

It still amazed Joe to think that he had been one of the first to witness the awful forces that had terrorized Millville. How could he have known what would follow? How could anybody? He had been that close—spitting distance, almost—and he was still alive. One of the lucky ones.

There were many unlucky ones. Before full-scale evacuation got underway people died fast and frequently. Even then the exodus was only a partial success. A considerable number of people, like Joe and Annie, simply refused to leave their homes.

If your number is up there's nothing you can do about it, Joe figured. He would rather sit in his own home and die if it came to that, than to flee like some wretched creature. He was too old to run.

As it happened, his neighborhood was not much damaged by the visitations. After Pachman's car was hit there were a few more attacks in nearby streets but nothing like the kind of trouble the rest of Millville had gone through. This was still a good old neighborhood.

What was the death toll? The amount of destruction in dollars? Joe had given up following the reports. Many and much, that was certain.

What was the nature of the beast? When it really started breaking loose Joe knew it could be only one thing. A warning. A warning and a reprimand. An act of God. Or Nature. It came to the same thing. All that other crap people talked about in the news was meaningless. Now that it had died down, more and more people were coming to see it the same way. The scientists could talk about unique environmental warps, backlashes, aberrations in force flow or any damn thing they liked. Maybe they weren't too far off, either, when it came to the nuts and bolts of the thing. But to Joe they were still missing the point. Would they learn? Not just about the terror, but about themselves too? That was what counted. Would they change or merely learn to cope?

This time had been a warning all right, a rap on the knuckles. Next time—who knows? To Joe it was all too clear. The lessons of great plagues and natural disasters were down in black and white in the Bible.

Maybe it was just as well, he thought. All things considered. He had seen a lot over the course of his life and as far as one man could tell the world was not getting any better. The trouble in Millville made him feel glad to be on the threshold of his old age. The golden years, they called them. Yeah, well… It seemed a pretty safe place to be.

The neighborhood was quiet this evening. Very few cars on the road. During the day people were wary enough, but at night even more so. Even the Italians across the way kept the television turned down low, as if too much noise might summon a reappearance of the terror. Who could tell? Give them credit anyhow, Joe thought. They stayed too.

Annie came down the hallway and stood by the screen door.

"You okay, Joe?"

"I'm fine, Annie."

"They had the news on. Ten o'clock."

"Yeah, what do they say?"

"Some people got killed in a building that was damaged out in Ohio. They don't know if it was an explosion or—"

"Like what we had?"

"Yeah, that's right. They think it might be."

"How about that," Joe said quietly.

"Want anything? Another beer?"

"No, I'm fine, Annie. I'll be in a little later."

"Okay, I'm going in to watch TV."

"Okay."

His wife disappeared inside.

So.

Maybe it's moved on, Joe thought. If that's the case, too bad for them.

Down the street a dog barked lazily.

About the Author

Thomas Tessier was born in Connecticut and educated there and at University College, Dublin. He lived in Dublin and London for thirteen years, during which time three books of his poems were published and three of his plays were professionally staged. For several years he wrote a monthly column on music for *Vogue* magazine (UK).

His short stories have appeared in numerous magazines and anthologies, including *Borderlands*, *Cemetery Dance*, *Prime Evil*, *Dark Terrors*, *The Year's Best Fantasy and Horror* and *Best New Horror*. His first collection of short fiction, *Ghost Music and Other Tales*, received an International Horror Guild Award. In 2013, his second collection, *Remorseless: Tales of Cruelty*, was published by Sinister Grin Press.

He is the author of several novels of terror and suspense, including *The Nightwalker*, *Phantom*, *Finishing Touches* and *Rapture*, which was made into a movie starring Karen Allen and Michael Ontkean. His novel *Fog Heart* received the International Horror Guild Award for Best Novel and was cited by *Publishers Weekly* as one of the best books of the year. His latest novel, *Wicked Things*, was published in paperback by Leisure Books and in hardcover by Cemetery Dance Publications.

Thomas Tessier lives in Connecticut. He is currently working on a new novel, as well as more short fiction.

Bibliography

Novels
Father Panic's Opera Macabre
Finishing Touches
Fog Heart
Phantom
Rapture

Secret Strangers
Shockwaves
The Fates
The Nightwalker
Wicked Things

<u>Short story collections</u>
Ghost Music and Other Tales
Remorseless: Tales of Cruelty

<u>Poetry collections</u>
Abandoned Homes
How We Died
In Sight of Chaos

Curious about other Crossroad Press books? Stop by our website:
http://crossroadpress.com
We offer quality writing
in digital, audio, and print formats.

Subscribe to our newsletter on the website homepage and receive a
free eBook.